FOREVER LOVED
THE FOREVER SERIES
BOOK SIX

AMANDA KIMBERLEY

Copyright © 2023 by Amanda Kimberley

All rights reserved.

No part of this book may be reproduced in any form or by any electronic or mechanical means, including information storage and retrieval systems, without written permission from the author, except for the use of brief quotations in a book review.

About Forever Loved

Eternal Love Is A Choice I Give You.

Raine and Skye, known as Djet and Aset in Forever Loved have spent countless lifetimes searching for each other. When they meet in each new reincarnation, they fall in love with each other all over again. But they say nothing is as good as the first time, and for them, their epic love always comes with an epic battle.

Will Raine and Skye manage to defeat Demetrese, the ruler of the underworld? Or will Demetrese send his army of demons to usurp the couple from their throne and doom the witches to an eternal life of rebirths and deaths?

In 300 B.C. in Egypt, there was only one certainty, free will, and a choice to love.

CHAPTER ONE

Lilith opened her eyes and sucked in her first breath as she took in all the purple blooms hanging from a vine in front of her. Warmth caressed her bare, umber skin, but she wasn't sure where the warmth was coming from just yet.

"She is beautiful. More than I could have ever dreamed, Jade Emperor Yudi!"

"I call her Lilith, Adam. And she is born from the same dust as you. She is your equal in every way. You will live together here in my garden as long as you wish."

Lilith shook her head. The words she was hearing seemed fuzzy. It was as if the voices were inside a cave, yet she wasn't cold, something she would expect in such a dank place. Words, their meanings, and speech seemed to flood her brain at a steady clip. Other knowledge, like companionship, humanity, and how she came to be, also seemed to swell her head.

"I promise to love her with all of my soul as you have asked me to, Yudi."

Warm and solid arms were now cradling her waist and hoisting her to an upright position. Still weak from awakening, Lilith fell into a chiseled torso that radiated heat so strong it was as if she was standing next to the sun itself. She screwed her eyes shut in fear of the light blinding her.

A hard object hit her inner thigh. She tried to shift her weight to ease the irritation penetrating her womanhood, but the more that she struggled against the pinch, the more she realized there wasn't much pain at all. In fact, desire seemed to replace the pain she initially experienced. She found her body responding to the wealth of pleasure growing deep within her belly. Her back arched, giving Adam a better entrance to her center. Lilith's fingers trailed down the length of Adam's back until they rested on his backside. Her hands instinctively cupped each cheek, and she ground his hips further into her core. Electric liquid heat coated them both as her inner lips pulsated around his cock. A faint moan escaped her before she bit her lip to dial back her increasing pleasure, now coming to her in waves.

"I will leave you both to grow my garden with

your children." Said the voice Lilith now knew belonged to Yudi.

The muscular arms that had lifted her to her feet were now guiding her down to a soft bed of leaves and vines.

"You are beautiful, Lilith, and you are all mine. I love you."

"I love you, too."

She reiterated the words strangely, like a parrot, and thought it silly at first. But she somehow knew what they meant without being told and thought the phrase was fitting. She did love this man. A man Yudi called Adam. A dull pain hit her belly again as something hard slipped between her thighs once more. The small hurt quickly turned into something pleasurable once more. She was becoming more and more aware of her surroundings as her hips rocked in union with Adam's. It was as if the fog was lifting from her brain and allowing her to think more clearly.

Her body soon stiffened as Adam's lips grazed her cheek. Adam recoiled quickly from her.

"I'm sorry! Am I doing something to hurt you? I don't mean to! Please tell me what it is you desire, and I will be forthright in obliging."

Lilith opened her eyes, and a person, whom she knew to be a man without question, was staring back at her. He had gorgeous green eyes. They were as verdant as the vines surrounding the two of them.

"You did nothing wrong. I'm still a bit confused. That's all. I'm not sure what to do or how to act. There's so much information to process."

"I understand. It was hard for me when Yudi made me."

"I understood the word as created. Is the phrase made you the same?"

"Yes, and he made you, too."

"And why did he make us?"

Adam shrugged his shoulders.

"He said he was lonely, so he made me for friendship and then created you for me so I'd have companionship as well. He wants us to have children, so this way, he's less lonely."

"Children?"

"Yes. Do you understand what those are? If not, it will come to you shortly. Yudi only gives you as much information as you can process within a moment's time. If you do not understand it now, you will see it shortly. But I will say that I can't wait to have babies with you and watch you care for them all."

"Babies? As in plural?"

Adam was right. The information was coming fast and hard, but Lilith wasn't sure if she liked Adam's viewpoint of the information. Was he that daft?

"And what will you be doing while I'm caring for our babies?"

"Forging for food, building us shelter, and gathering wood for a fire. It is my job to care for you, protect you and the babies in these ways."

"We are equals—are we not?"

"Of course."

"Then why are you the one that forges for food? Can't I do the same?"

"Who will provide the babies with nourishment in your absence?"

Lilith sucked in a breath. She wanted to protest, but as more information flooded her mind, she realized Adam was right.

Damn it.

No one could provide nourishment for the babies in her absence. Her chest was the only thing that could give the babes milk.

How is this fair? How is it equal?

The answer he provided bothered her. Sure, she was a woman and could do things he could not, but that didn't mean they weren't equal in other ways. He grew so adamant about having a protective hold over her, and right now, it seemed... Stifling. So stifling, she shifted her weight away from him.

"I'll be back. I want to go for a swim."

It was the first excuse she could think of to get away from him and collect her thoughts. Thoughts that seemed to crowd over her like a shadow, keeping her down and pliable to do whatever Adam and her creator asked of her.

"I will join you shortly. I want to collect wood for a fire so you don't get cold once you finish your swim."

He rose and turned on his heel and headed for the forest to gather the wood. Lilith jumped into the water, and a sense of calm washed over her once the water surrounded her. She knew Adam wasn't a bad person. He really did care for her and even said he loved her. Adam just seemed misguided about equality, and Lilith hoped she could change that by having a chat with Yudi. Surely Yudi will understand the importance of her and Adam being equal partners in this companionship he'd concocted in his god-like mind.

THE SUN WAS ALREADY SINKING DOWN on the horizon when Adam returned.

This forging takes a prolonged amount of time. I'm uncertain that I like the idea of him being away from me for so long.

Adam swam towards her. She felt her core quicken with desire again as his hooded gaze met hers. She bit her bottom lip as her eyes gazed upon his dark, chiseled chest and bulging biceps. When he finally reached her, he wrapped an arm around her waist to pull the length of her body against his. With his free hand, he cupped her cheek and traced a line over her bottom lip with his hard, calloused thumb.

"It drives me crazy when you do that, love. It makes me want to fill you with my seed so we can have many babies together."

Lilith sucked in a shaky breath before Adam's lips crashed down on hers. He parted the seam with his tongue and explored her mouth. Lilith laced her fingers through Adam's thick, dark locks. She hoped it was a sign to him that she enjoyed this intimacy he was currently giving to her. His lips trailed to her chin, neck, and collarbone before they kissed the tops of each breast. He then cupped her right breast and took it in his mouth, sucking on the nipple. Heat rushed directly to her lower belly.

"You are so beautiful, Lilith, and are mine in every way. I want nothing more than to give you the pleasure you deserve."

Lilith cupped his cheeks and rubbed her thumbs along his rugged jawline. She couldn't help but smile at the man. Sure, she wasn't sure about his over-protectiveness, but it was indeed coming from a love that she could be sure of.

"Come with me. I've gathered wood for a fire and some fruit for a meal. Tomorrow morning, I will leave at first light to hunt for a wild game so we can have a feast and celebrate our union."

Adam was already gone when Lilith awoke. She settled on gathering some kindling and wood for the fire pit Adam had made yesterday evening. Once she was done, Lilith cleaned around the fire area to clear away hard pebbles that were digging into the soles of her feet. She stepped back and smiled, pleased with her work. Next, she added the wood to the fire so it would be ready to cook whatever game Adam was hunting for. The sun was leaning toward the horizon when Adam returned with a deer.

She smiled as he approached, but his gaze lowered from hers as he rushed to embrace her. And instead of pulling her into his muscular arms, he cupped her breasts instead.

"I've missed you, woman. Come, let's celebrate my kill by taking a bath together in the water."

His grip was gentle but firm on her chest, something she was used to, but only while they were making love, and never before had he held and kissed her in his arms in his greeting. This possessiveness seemed different. For the first time since Yudi breathed life into her, she wasn't sure if she liked the proprietorial hold Yudi gave Adam over her. Sure, Adam was a male and practically a different species than her. He spoke before he thought and mostly reacted to the things around him rather than acting accordingly. At least, as far as she was concerned, anyway. Adam always had an opinion about how she did something, and lately, that didn't settle well with her.

Lilith contemplated the issue at hand before she ever spoke a word. She understood Yudi gave her this gift to compliment Adam's alpha approach to the world around him. All of it made sense to Lilith. Adam and his sons she'd raise with him would need the alpha and cunning behavior to hunt wild animals for food. They needed these gifts to help them all survive.

But Lilith still wished he could turn off that possessive alpha part of his brain when he came home to her, especially since she was trying to become the woman Adam wanted and needed once he returned from a long day of hunting. She didn't think she was asking for too much—a simple give-and-take was all she needed to feel special and appreciated.

"You must be tired from your journey—why don't you rest, and I'll make some stew from the meat."

Lilith placed a hand on Adam's chest and tried to gently put some distance between them, but he wrapped his arms around her tighter.

"Nonsense! We will bathe together, and I will

make love to my Lilith, so you know how loved and adored you are."

His eyes were dark as they raked over her body. This seemed to become more and more of a ritual, with him claiming her. Usually, she didn't mind. Despite his Neanderthal ways of doing things, she knew he cared about her. But all she wanted to do was crawl up into a little ball next to him and sleep for days. She craved that type of intimacy with him this evening.

He was making her feel strange tonight, just as he had for the previous two. Each night he'd come back to their dwelling later and later, complaining about the hunt for food taking longer and longer than the day before. He'd often come home immediately after his fresh kill and wanted to celebrate with wine, food, and love-making.

But tonight wasn't a time that Lilith wanted him to think merely of himself. Especially after his eyes darkened like he was viewing her as an object he possessed rather than a woman he cared for and treasured. He scooped her up in his arms, and as soon as he placed her in the water, his hands pawed at her chest. They seemed to have a mind of their own as they seared her skin and branded hers as Adam's.

"Adam, please. Let's enjoy some dinner and conversation first."

She didn't mind his possessive touch. It made

her feel wanted and needed. But tonight, all she wanted was a doting, tender touch.

His body grew ridged, and his eyes screwed shut before he sucked in a breath.

"I'm sorry. Does my holding you not please you? I can be more gentle."

His hands trailed from her breasts up her arms and shoulders before cupping her cheeks. A warmth washed over her as electric heat prickled her skin from his touch. It immediately changed from possessive to doting and loving, and Lilith found herself melting into a puddle of mush that resembled the fruit she'd been mashing up for her babes to eat earlier in the day. Her emotions went from course to sweet in a matter of seconds once Adam went from grinding his hips into her inner thighs to brushing the tip of his manhood over her entrance. Her lips curled as he touched them with his own.

Adam brushed her lips with his once more before sucking on her bottom lip. The sensation was a mixture of the feather of a dove grazing her lips before a fish from the river she bathed in nuzzled at her ankles. Such a tender touch, something she'd been craving from him for the past three moons, and if she hadn't tasted the sweat on his upper lip, a gorgeous blend of rain and sea, she would have thought he didn't touch her lips at all. He'd become that in tune with her within seconds. Lilith, for the first time in a while, understood why Yudi called the

Garden of Eden a paradise. Everything seemed to be falling into place.

Finally.

"I love the taste of you. It's a sweet combination of gentle rain and the unpredictable sea."

His eyes softened, and a smile spread across his face before one of his large hands encompassed her right cheek.

"I'm glad my sometimes unpredictability pleases you."

"It does."

"I love you, Lilith."

"And I love you."

Adam was gone all day again. It had been 7 full moons since their last perfect night together, and Lilith was beginning to wonder if Adam would only please her if she were stubborn about explaining to him what she needed. Today though? She was too tired even to try. She'd fallen into a fitful sleep waiting for him to come home, and when he got back, he expected Lilith to spend the entire evening with him. After spending all day caring for the children, Lilith was too tired to function. Even with Aset, an immortal witch who was brought to Lilith to help, Lilith was still too tired to move. She wasn't sure how she could will her body to make love to Adam.

"Baby, I've missed you. It's lonely hunting all day, and I want to be with you tonight."

"And I'm tired. I tended to the babies all day. I've been poked, prodded, and wearing caked-on spit-up. All I want to do is bathe and fall asleep."

Adam cupped her cheek. She peered into his eyes and saw sympathy. It was a welcome change to be on the receiving end rather than being the one having to dish out the fondness she held for Adam.

"Of course, my darling. Do what you have to. I'll tend to the babes and put them down for their evening nap."

She patted Adam's hand, which was still on her cheek.

"Thank you, Adam. This means so much."

"Certainly! After all, you need a break from your motherly responsibilities. I will have Aset help me."

"Aset has been helping me all day, too. She's also tired."

"I'm sure she won't mind a few more minutes."

Adam walked off before Lilith could say anything more. She knew Yudi made her for Adam. She was supposed to be Adam's perfect match, but there were times, especially now, when Lilith felt that was so far from the truth. Lilith knew she couldn't put it off anymore. She had to talk to Yudi.

CHAPTER TWO

Lilith opened her eyes and sucked in her first breath as she took in all the purple blooms hanging from a vine in front of her. Warmth caressed her bare, umber skin, but she wasn't sure where the warmth was coming from just yet.

"She is beautiful. More than I could have ever dreamed, Jade Emperor Yudi!"

"I call her Lilith, Adam. And she is born from the same dust as you. She is your equal in every way. You will live together here in my garden as long as you wish."

Lilith shook her head. The words she was hearing seemed fuzzy. It was as if the voices were inside a cave, yet she wasn't cold, something she would expect in such a dank place. Words, their meanings, and speech seemed to flood her brain at a steady clip. Other knowledge, like companionship, humanity, and how she came to be, also seemed to swell her head.

"I promise to love her with all of my soul as you have asked me to, Yudi."

Warm and solid arms were now cradling her waist and hoisting her to an upright position. Still weak from awakening, Lilith fell into a chiseled torso that radiated heat so strong it was as if she was standing next to the sun itself. She screwed her eyes shut in fear of the light blinding her.

A hard object hit her inner thigh. She tried to shift her weight to ease the irritation penetrating her womanhood, but the more that she struggled against the pinch, the more she realized there wasn't much pain at all. In fact, desire seemed to replace the pain she initially experienced. She found her body responding to the wealth of pleasure growing deep within her belly. Her back arched, giving Adam a better entrance to her center. Lilith's fingers trailed down the length of Adam's back until they rested on his backside. Her hands instinctively cupped each cheek, and she ground his hips further into her core. Electric liquid heat coated them both as her inner lips pulsated around his cock. A faint moan escaped her before she bit her lip to dial back her increasing pleasure, now coming to her in waves.

"I will leave you both to grow my garden with

your children." Said the voice Lilith now knew belonged to Yudi.

The muscular arms that had lifted her to her feet were now guiding her down to a soft bed of leaves and vines.

"You are beautiful, Lilith, and you are all mine. I love you."

"I love you, too."

She reiterated the words strangely, like a parrot, and thought it silly at first. But she somehow knew what they meant without being told and thought the phrase was fitting. She did love this man. A man Yudi called Adam. A dull pain hit her belly again as something hard slipped between her thighs once more. The small hurt quickly turned into something pleasurable once more. She was becoming more and more aware of her surroundings as her hips rocked in union with Adam's. It was as if the fog was lifting from her brain and allowing her to think more clearly.

Her body soon stiffened as Adam's lips grazed her cheek. Adam recoiled quickly from her.

"I'm sorry! Am I doing something to hurt you? I don't mean to! Please tell me what it is you desire, and I will be forthright in obliging."

Lilith opened her eyes, and a person, whom she knew to be a man without question, was staring back at her. He had gorgeous green eyes. They were as verdant as the vines surrounding the two of them.

"You did nothing wrong. I'm still a bit confused. That's all. I'm not sure what to do or how to act. There's so much information to process."

"I understand. It was hard for me when Yudi made me."

"I understood the word as created. Is the phrase made you the same?"

"Yes, and he made you, too."

"And why did he make us?"

Adam shrugged his shoulders.

"He said he was lonely, so he made me for friendship and then created you for me so I'd have companionship as well. He wants us to have children, so this way, he's less lonely."

"Children?"

"Yes. Do you understand what those are? If not, it will come to you shortly. Yudi only gives you as much information as you can process within a moment's time. If you do not understand it now, you will see it shortly. But I will say that I can't wait to have babies with you and watch you care for them all."

"Babies? As in plural?"

Adam was right. The information was coming fast and hard, but Lilith wasn't sure if she liked Adam's viewpoint of the information. Was he that daft?

"And what will you be doing while I'm caring for our babies?"

"Forging for food, building us shelter, and gathering wood for a fire. It is my job to care for you, protect you and the babies in these ways."

"We are equals—are we not?"

"Of course."

"Then why are you the one that forges for food? Can't I do the same?"

"Who will provide the babies with nourishment in your absence?"

Lilith sucked in a breath. She wanted to protest, but as more information flooded her mind, she realized Adam was right.

Damn it.

No one could provide nourishment for the babies in her absence. Her chest was the only thing that could give the babes milk.

How is this fair? How is it equal?

The answer he provided bothered her. Sure, she was a woman and could do things he could not, but that didn't mean they weren't equal in other ways. He grew so adamant about having a protective hold over her, and right now, it seemed... Stifling. So stifling, she shifted her weight away from him.

"I'll be back. I want to go for a swim."

It was the first excuse she could think of to get away from him and collect her thoughts. Thoughts that seemed to crowd over her like a shadow, keeping her down and pliable to do whatever Adam and her creator asked of her.

"I will join you shortly. I want to collect wood for a fire so you don't get cold once you finish your swim."

He rose and turned on his heel and headed for the forest to gather the wood. Lilith jumped into the water, and a sense of calm washed over her once the water surrounded her. She knew Adam wasn't a bad person. He really did care for her and even said he loved her. Adam just seemed misguided about equality, and Lilith hoped she could change that by having a chat with Yudi. Surely Yudi will understand the importance of her and Adam being equal partners in this companionship he'd concocted in his god-like mind.

THE SUN WAS ALREADY SINKING DOWN on the horizon when Adam returned.

This forging takes a prolonged amount of time. I'm uncertain that I like the idea of him being away from me for so long.

Adam swam towards her. She felt her core quicken with desire again as his hooded gaze met hers. She bit her bottom lip as her eyes gazed upon his dark, chiseled chest and bulging biceps. When he finally reached her, he wrapped an arm around her waist to pull the length of her body against his. With his free hand, he cupped her cheek and traced a line over her bottom lip with his hard, calloused thumb.

"It drives me crazy when you do that, love. It makes me want to fill you with my seed so we can have many babies together."

Lilith sucked in a shaky breath before Adam's lips crashed down on hers. He parted the seam with his tongue and explored her mouth. Lilith laced her fingers through Adam's thick, dark locks. She hoped it was a sign to him that she enjoyed this intimacy he was currently giving to her. His lips trailed to her chin, neck, and collarbone before they kissed the tops of each breast. He then cupped her right breast and took it in his mouth, sucking on the nipple. Heat rushed directly to her lower belly.

"You are so beautiful, Lilith, and are mine in every way. I want nothing more than to give you the pleasure you deserve."

Lilith cupped his cheeks and rubbed her thumbs along his rugged jawline. She couldn't help but smile at the man. Sure, she wasn't sure about his over-protectiveness, but it was indeed coming from a love that she could be sure of.

"Come with me. I've gathered wood for a fire and some fruit for a meal. Tomorrow morning, I will leave at first light to hunt for a wild game so we can have a feast and celebrate our union."

Garden of Eden a paradise. Everything seemed to be falling into place.

Finally.

"I love the taste of you. It's a sweet combination of gentle rain and the unpredictable sea."

His eyes softened, and a smile spread across his face before one of his large hands encompassed her right cheek.

"I'm glad my sometimes unpredictability pleases you."

"It does."

"I love you, Lilith."

"And I love you."

ADAM WAS GONE all day again. It had been 7 full moons since their last perfect night together, and Lilith was beginning to wonder if Adam would only please her if she were stubborn about explaining to him what she needed. Today though? She was too tired even to try. She'd fallen into a fitful sleep waiting for him to come home, and when he got back, he expected Lilith to spend the entire evening with him. After spending all day caring for the children, Lilith was too tired to function. Even with Aset, an immortal witch who was brought to Lilith to help, Lilith was still too tired to move. She wasn't sure how she could will her body to make love to Adam.

"Baby, I've missed you. It's lonely hunting all day, and I want to be with you tonight."

"And I'm tired. I tended to the babies all day. I've been poked, prodded, and wearing caked-on spit-up. All I want to do is bathe and fall asleep."

Adam cupped her cheek. She peered into his eyes and saw sympathy. It was a welcome change to be on the receiving end rather than being the one having to dish out the fondness she held for Adam.

"Of course, my darling. Do what you have to. I'll tend to the babes and put them down for their evening nap."

She patted Adam's hand, which was still on her cheek.

"Thank you, Adam. This means so much."

"Certainly! After all, you need a break from your motherly responsibilities. I will have Aset help me."

"Aset has been helping me all day, too. She's also tired."

"I'm sure she won't mind a few more minutes."

Adam walked off before Lilith could say anything more. She knew Yudi made her for Adam. She was supposed to be Adam's perfect match, but there were times, especially now, when Lilith felt that was so far from the truth. Lilith knew she couldn't put it off anymore. She had to talk to Yudi.

CHAPTER
THREE

"Don't you see it?" Lilith asked as she let out a breath of exasperation.

"Babe, I'm nothing like your ex Adam. He's a human, a meager mortal now that he's been cast out of Eden. I've nothing in common with someone like him."

"Then why must you assume I cannot handle ruling over your demons? Yudi put me in charge of the seven planes of existence. Can't I relieve you of some of your burdens with the Underworld realm? I mean—isn't that what partners are supposed to do?"

"Babe," Demetrese said as he stroked Lilith's silky pin-straight ebony hair before continuing. "Yudi entrusted me to rule over the seven realms of the Underworld, which is similar to ruling over seven planes—don't get me wrong—I understand that. We are equal partners in that, and it's not that I don't want the help—I merely don't want to burden you. You have so much to create in your planes. Yudi didn't leave you much instruction. He just told you to create planes suitable for the magical creatures that will live there."

"He asked the same of you."

"Yes, he did."

"So? Can't I help you collaborate ideas for your realms like you've helped me with my planes?"

Demetrese took her hand and patted it.

"My darling, perhaps later? Right now, I'd rather spend time with you and talk about anything else but work. Creating something from nothing is exhausting, you know that."

"I do. And that is why I wish to relieve you of some of the burdens."

"You can help me by allowing me the pleasure of some good conversation over a bottle of fine wine and a lovely dinner. Amon has made Chateau Briand for us both."

Lilith smiled slightly before lowering her head. Sure, Demetrese wasn't the same as Adam—hell, he seemed a thousand percent better than the Neanderthal she left back in Eden. But something still didn't seem right. Demetrese seemed distant and standoffish whenever she brought up Yudi and her residing over the seven planes, a reign that included earth. All of it was a bit more complex than his ruling over just the Underworld. At least, that's how she perceived it. But? Perhaps she was overthinking it all?

After all, Adam's bruteness and Demetrese's tender side were like night and day in comparison. And Demetrese had told her that she could help him collaborate in the future. He just seemed to want to relax, which is something that Lilith could get behind. Because she, too, was tired after creating the woodland area for fairies in the spiritual plane today. So many trees, mushrooms, little houses, and shinies. It was maddening!

He poured her a glass of Bordeaux and handed it to her while sporting an easy smile.

"I enjoy spending time with you. It helps me relax after a long day."

"I feel the same way too."

She found herself smiling back as easily as he was. Her reservations were almost a distant memory as he clinked his glass with hers.

"Here's to many more fond memories to come."

"I second that."

"Good. Now let's put the troubles of the day behind us, and let me pamper you by drawing you a bath and giving you a massage."

Lilith's eyes widened as a warmth encircled her body. Never had Adam pampered her in any way before, and especially not like this. In fact, he expected her to be the one providing the pampering because of her caring, maternal nature.

But this? It was different and completely out of her comfort zone. Sure, she'd hated Adam's domineering side, but it was familiar, predictable. She wasn't sure if she wanted to shed her mask and become vulnerable to Demetrese's touch—a touch she'd been craving all day. She lowered her eyes before responding to him.

"You don't have to go through all that trouble for me. I can take care of myself."

Demetrese placed his wine goblet down on the table and got up to meet Lilith. "Don't you see it?" Lilith asked as she let out a breath of exasperation.

"Babe, I'm nothing like your ex, Adam. He's a human, a meager mortal, now on earth after Yudi's cast him out of Eden and all. I've nothing in common with someone like him, and you should be happy you aren't even in the same realm as he is."

"Babe," Demetrese said as he stroked Lilith's silky, pin-straight ebony hair before continuing. "Yudi entrusted me to rule over the seven realms of the Underworld, which is similar to ruling over seven planes—don't get me wrong—because I understand that. We are partners in that, and it's not that I don't want the help. I merely don't want to burden you. You have so much to create in your planes. Yudi didn't leave you much instruction. He just told you to create planes suitable for the magical creatures that will live there."

"He asked the same of you."

"Yes, he did."

"So? Can't I help you collaborate ideas for your realms like you've helped me with my planes?"

Demetrese took her hand and patted it.

"My darling, perhaps later? Right now, I'd rather spend time with you and talk about anything else but work. Creating something from nothing is exhausting, you know that."

"I do. And that is why I wish to relieve you of some of those burdens."

"You can help me by allowing me the pleasure of some delightful conversation over a bottle of fine wine and a lovely dinner. Amon has made Chateaubriand for us both."

Lilith smiled slightly before lowering her head. Sure, Demetrese wasn't the same as Adam—hell, he seemed a thousand percent better than the Neanderthal she left back in Eden. But something still didn't seem right. Demetrese seemed distant and standoffish whenever she brought up Yudi and her residing over the seven planes, a reign that included earth. All of it was a bit more complex than his ruling over just the Underworld and the realms contained within them. At least, that's how she perceived it. But? Perhaps she was overthinking it all?

After all, Adam's brutish and Demetrese's tender sides were like night and day in comparison. And Demetrese had told her she could help him collaborate in the future. He just seemed to want to relax, which is something that Lilith could get behind. Because she, too, was tired after creating the woodland area for fairies in the magical spiritual plane today. So many trees, mushrooms, tiny houses, and those darn "shinies." It was maddening!

He poured her a glass of Bordeaux and handed it to her while sporting a serene smile.

"I enjoy spending time with you. It helps me relax after a long day."

"I feel the same way, too."

She found it easy to smile back. Seemed as easy as sipping the wine and enjoying herself. Her reservations were almost a distant memory as he clinked his glass with hers.

"Here's to many more fond memories to come."

"I second that." She drew the goblet to her lips. The wine was a smooth, dry combination, exactly how she liked it.

"Good. Now let's put the troubles of the day behind us. Let me pamper you by drawing you a bath and giving you a massage."

Lilith's eyes widened as a warmth encircled her body. Never had Adam pampered her before, and especially not like this. In fact, he expected her to be the one providing the pampering because of her caring, maternal, unconditionally loving nature.

But this? It was different and completely out of her comfort zone. Sure, she'd hated Adam's domineering side, but it was familiar, predictable. She wasn't sure if she wanted to shed her mask and become vulnerable to Demetrese's touch—a touch she'd been craving all day. She lowered her eyes before responding to him—because why wouldn't she? This relationship—or whatever it was brooding between them seemed to develop far too fast for her liking. They hadn't kissed. They hadn't even slept in the same bed yet. Yup! He created a bedroom just for her that first night. Which honestly? She loved it and was grateful for it. He was patient with her, something she didn't think was a possible trait for a man to possess.

"You don't have to go through all that trouble for me. I can take care of myself."

The words were meant to come out kind—not harsh, yet her teeth clenched as she'd said them.

Demetrese placed his wine goblet down on the table and got up to meet Lilith. He lifted her chin with his index finger.

"Stand up, Lilith." He said to her in a buttery soft tone—which was nothing she deserved after her angry tone with him.

He tucked a few stray strands of hair behind her ear as she stood. "There. That's better. I like my equal looking at me in the eyes when I'm talking. Lilith, I understand you can do things by yourself, but you don't have to now. You've got me. So please, let me take care of you and help you relax."

Lilith swore she heard him let out a long breath, but it was gone as fast as his hand was around her ear.

"This isn't sexual. Let me care for you."

Lilith smiled brightly as he drew her forehead to hers. How was it possible to have a man in her life that didn't look at her as pure sex? She couldn't believe how lucky she was to have Demetrese in her life. And? For the first time since she'd been in the Underworld, she was happy that Yudi suggested she spend time with Demetrese. It had only been a week, so Lilith would not get her hopes up. However, this was undoubtedly a good start.

CHAPTER FOUR

She asked her best friend to help her dress because this was the first time he had ever invited her to the palace alone. She'd been to a couple of parties that followed Djet's coronation. But aside from the occasional glance, Djet kept his distance so as not to perpetuate the rumors already circulating throughout the court about them consummating their relationship before marriage.

Aset wasn't sure if he'd done that solely on her part or not. She was adamant with him they should keep up appearances. Especially since he was considered a young ruler. Young rulers can be usurped so easily, and Aset didn't want that for Djet.

Her village had talked about her powerful psychic visions, and that won the intrigue of the court of the newly appointed king of Egypt. But their flirting with one another was the true talk of the court. Aset wasn't perfect by any stretch of the means, but she didn't much care for others talking about her and Djet. Especially not when it could get him killed.

Aset had known Djet since the beginning because Yudi made them immortal witches to aid Lilith in the Garden of Eden. The gods were kind to them both once they were the first witches ever created. Both she and Djet took on Lilith's characteristics, powers, and personality.

All of Lilith's powers had perks, but the gift of immortality was the greatest of them all for a witch. Every spell and prayer was far more potent than the rituals or prayers any mortal sorcerer performed. It was why the gods' one absolute law was that no witch could perform magic on a mortal, especially Djet and Aset, because they were the first and most powerful.

This law was stricter than any they had in Eden, and Aset often missed her carefree days because being cast out as a pariah hurt more than anything she'd ever experienced until now. Earth would be different, of course, having its own set of rules she didn't understand just yet.

Being Lilith's proverbial firsts, Lilith had a great fondness for both her and Djet and always told them they'd be a perfect match for each other when the time came to take on mates. The thought was always strange to Aset because she had hoped to find a connection outside the small circle the Garden of Eden provided. But since she and Djet were the first witches created, it wasn't long for her to figure out they were made for each other—much like her mother was supposedly made for Adam.

It must have been why it was so easy to gaze upon Djet's masculine body. His chiseled chest boasted he was a powerful leader. And each hard plane was surely pleasant to look at. But Aset found it more enticing to talk with him. She enjoyed speaking with him because the more he confided in her, the closer she appeared to be to him.

A sensation, much like watching butterflies flutter in the air, always made its way to her belly when Djet sat next to her in court. And oh, how she wished she knew she was making the right decision by pursuing Djet. Sure, Lilith thought it was a good idea—heck, the gods probably did too, for all she knew! But with what happened to the first woman she cared for, to their Lilith once the gods sentenced them all because of Adam? That made Aset fear for her future on earth.

Everything changed the minute Adam stopped listening to Lilith's wishes and left her to fend for herself with an ever-growing brood of babies, all needing sustenance and love. Yudi, an all-loving (supposedly) and all-knowing god, made both Lilith and Adam and the glorious Garden of Eden. However, Yudi didn't pass down the power of omnipresence to Lilith. Instead, Yudi thought Adam would be better equipped with such a powerful skill since he anticipated Adam would require it while hunting for food.

And seriously? What man on earth wouldn't want the power to multi-task while forging for sustenance? It was a powerful skill to have, indeed! Yudi granted Lilith the ability to love every being created, imagined, or present unconditionally. This meant that anyone or anything on the earth or other planes of existence would be protected by Lilith because she would be the creator of such planes. Yudi believed Lilith's ability to love unconditionally was her greatest gift to her children and humanity. And all worked well. They all lived in harmony for thousands of centuries, as Yudi intended.

However, when Lilith fled Eden, all proverbial hell broke loose. Adam rescinded his love within an hour of her running from their fight and demanded that Yudi make another companion for him—this time, one that was obedient.

Aset grew weary of the new Eden and couldn't see a place for herself there either, especially once the other gods asked her to live in Egypt and help them with tragic times outside of Eden on earth. Sadly, Yudi didn't want to face Aset himself, which was why he had Isis do the asking. Aset went but with reluctance because she didn't want to leave Djet. He may have been male and impervious to

Yudi's wrath, but that didn't mean Aset wasn't worried.

She was sad when she was told Djet wouldn't follow her until later, but she had hoped they'd reunite quickly. They'd been best friends and so close they finished each other's thoughts while living together in Eden. And that was probably why Aset found no companionship quite like Djet, so she lived in Egypt alone, having only herself as her best company until the day she saw Djet in the palace. Her heart skipped a beat when they first made eye contact.

She was anxious as she prepared to meet him again now that it was 300 BC in Egypt. The rules seemed different because they were no longer under their pseudo-parents' or Yudi's thumb in Eden. That very thought seemed more true as Aset recalled the last time she saw Djet. He didn't speak to her, but his gaze was hooded as she walked past him in court. And electric heat seemed to beam off of each of them, even if they were on opposite ends of the room. Aset couldn't help but imagine what heat would generate between them if he held her in his arms.

They could do and be to each other what pleased them as immortal witches on earth. No one had the authority to give them rules because they'd be the most powerful beings on the earth plane. At least, that was according to Isis. Yudi didn't tell them otherwise, but that was probably because he chickened out and had Isis be the bearer of bad news for them both.

As far as Aset was concerned, she intended to live life to the fullest now that her best friend had joined her in Egypt. A flash of Djet's sexy smile entered her mind, and the thought made her stomach do a couple of flip-flops. She'd never thought of him as sexy when they were in Eden. Probably because they were both too busy helping Lilith. But now? It seemed his dark chocolate eyes, chiseled chest, and broad shoulders were all she thought about.

She made her way to the grand hall in an Egyptian palace built specifically for Djet. It was strange to be personally escorted by his royal guards. She was an ordinary being, and with each passing gilded adornment on the walls, as they walked, she realized just how common she was compared to Djet. The guards opened the doors to the meeting room, and she was greeted by that sexy smile she'd come accustomed to seeing on her dear Djet. Her heart pounded profusely and seemed to want to push right out of her chest. Aset took in a few deep breaths to try to steady her heart rate and calm her wobbling legs.

"It's good to see you, Aset. Was your trip to the palace pleasant?" He pulled her into his arms. But Aset pulled away after a few seconds, worried that her heart, which now was slamming up against her rib cage, would betray her. She looked away from Djet as heat rushed through her cheeks.

"Yes. The ride was very comfortable, but you didn't need to send your carriage for me."

"Nothing but the best for my Aset! Would you care for some wine?" Djet said as he reached for an empty goblet.

One of his servants, a young girl with pin-straight dark locks, rushed to his side with a bottle.

"Sire, let me pour the wine for you."

"Nonsense, Oni, I am more than capable of serving Aset myself. In fact, please leave us. I wish to catch up with my best friend alone."

Aset lowered her gaze again. But this time, instead of her heart slamming against her chest cavity, it had stopped. Her stomach bottomed out as well. The thought of him calling her his friend didn't sit well with her. At least not anymore.

Not after he looked at her with longing in his eyes at the parties. And certainly not now, as the depths seemed to exude his neediness for something more from her. She saw him as a man—and a sexy one at that—and the term friend really didn't fit. Djet walked up to her after the servants and guards left. He offered the goblet with one hand and lifted her chin with the other.

"I prefer to see your beautiful eyes when I'm speaking with you."

He cupped her cheek, and his gaze darkened as he stroked her cheek with his thumb. Electric heat seared her skin with each stroke. It was as if he was marking her with each pass of his thumb. Branding her so everyone knew she was his. Aset's throat grew to bone-dry proportions, and her gaze automatically drew to the floor as his eyes grew impossibly darker.

"Don't do that, sweetness. I told you I wish to experience the glint in your eyes as I speak with you. That glint tells me if we are both in unison." He said as he tapped her cheek before continuing. "Have I upset you? If so, please say how so I may correct it. Because I never want to be out of sequence with you."

The term of endearment he used was nice. Aset had to admit to herself that her stomach did a backflip while hearing his voice go husky on the one word. But she was still hung up on the first choice word he'd used.

Aset placed a palm on his rock-hard chest that seemed to tighten more under her touch. She then put some distance between the two of them. There was no way she was going to have this type of conversation with someone who thought of her as only a friend.

"Nothing's wrong. Everything is fine."

He wrapped an arm around her waist and pulled her close.

"Then why are you pushing me away when I wish nothing more than to be close to you?"

Aset sucked in a breath as she felt him harden against her inner thigh. His hand trailed up and down her back, leaving goosebumps with every pass. She bit her lip in an attempt not to moan at his touch. But if he didn't stop caressing her lower back with his hand dangerously close to her backside soon, all bets were off that she'd remain a chaste woman.

"Aset, I've missed you so, so much. I haven't been able to get you out of my mind. There's nothing more I desire than for you to be in my life now and always."

He pulled her into his arms and rested his head on her shoulder.

"All I can think about is kissing your soft skin."

Aset sucked in another breath as Djet's lips brushed her neck.

"Will you let me kiss your lips, Aset? I want to see if they are as soft as the skin on your neck. Please, sweetness."

His lips were hovering over her ear, tickling her skin with his hot breath.

"Yes."

It was all she could say before her mouth went dry again.

His lips brushed her jawline and cheek before they brushed over her own. The kiss was soft at first and then deepened as his tongue traced the outline of her seam to part them. A soft moan escaped her lips, and she felt Djet's lips form a smile over her skin. He pulled back from her, and her body mourned his searing touch until he cupped both of her cheeks.

"I've been wanting to kiss you since the first time I saw you at the palace for my coronation." He pressed his forehead against hers. "Sweetness, I can't live another minute apart from you. Will you stay with me at the palace and become my wife?"

Aset searched his eyes, questioning her own ears. Sure, she'd wanted him to look at her as more than someone he'd been with in Eden. She even wondered what it would be like if she were his wife, but she never thought that he'd actually ask.

"Are you sure?"

The words escaped her lips because everything he was saying was such a shock, so much so that she questioned his sanity.

"Of course, I'm sure. You are my best friend, the best oracle in all the world, and hopefully, you will become my lover and consort once we marry. Now that I'm king, I only want the people around me I can trust. I know I can trust you, sweetness. It's all I've ever wanted. Well, that and exclusivity. If you become my wife, I'll only be with you. There will no longer be a harem in the palace as long as I reign over Egypt."

Now she really thought he was delusional. What king only has one wife these days? Certainly not one that she'd ever known.

"There will no longer be a harem in the palace?"

It was silly to repeat his words. It sounded like she was his echo, but she was still having trouble grasping everything he was saying. He wrapped his arm around her waist and pulled her close. She felt his hard length pressing against her inner thigh again and bit back a moan.

"Sweetness, you are all that I need."

His lips were on hers the instant he finished the sentence. The kiss scorched her body, filling every nerve ending with its heat as he sucked on her bottom lip. A whimper that she didn't entirely give permission to escape her did as his hands glided down her back and hooked around her waist.

"And you are mine. All mine."

Her breath hitched at his possessive declaration. Then his palms slid further down her back to cup her backside. She let out a yelp, which was more out of surprise than it was out of excitement. She placed her palms against his chest and gave him a gentle push to put some distance between them so she could meet his eyes. They were still hooded and dark pools, speaking more words than his actions had.

"Djet, what if the court sees us?"

He tucked a few loose strands of hair behind her ear before cupping both her cheeks, pinning her gaze to his for a longer-than-normal second before responding.

"Let them see that I'm crazy about you, sweetheart. We are about to marry. No one will blame us for being in love."

"The humans love to talk about us, though. It makes me uncomfortable. They seem to be pettier than Yudi."

"Sweetness, we are not them, and nor will we ever be. Goddess Isis blessed this union, and I love you with all that I am and all that I will become. Forget about what others say. Especially my human subjects, because you are right. They are all petty. Pettier than the gods they worship. All will be wonderful once I make you my wife. You will see."

He cupped her cheek and brushed her forehead with his lips. The gesture was so soft that it made Aset's knees buckle.

"I hope you are right. It's just I have this nagging feeling."

He smoothed out her hair.

"And when you come to understand what that feeling you have is psychically, we will deal with it. Okay?"

He pressed his forehead to hers and pulled her waist back to his.

"Okay."

"I mean it, sweetness. Don't worry about

anything in the future. Just look forward to becoming my wife."

He tapped her backside, causing her to squeal again—only this time, it was with delight. Her eyes flew open and met his gaze. Djet's pupils covered almost all the dark chocolate brown Aset loved staring back at. Especially lately because there was so much passion in his eyes when he gazed at her. These eyes were filled with a desire for her and only her. His mouth was claiming hers now, and not in a needy fashion, but a possessive one as his lips sucked on her top one, and hard.

Djet's hands ran down her back until they were cupping her backside once more, and then he pulled her waist closer to his. A heat Aset hadn't known in her entire life began to swell deep within her belly. The intensity was so powerful that her knees gave out, but Djet's muscular arms held her in place.

"Hey," Djet said as he tapped Aset's backside once more.

Aset flicked her eyes open.

"What?"

"Please look at me. I want to see your eyes fill with want and need when I pleasure you."

His lips trailed down her neck to the valley between her breasts. All the while, his eyes were locked on her, pinning her gaze in place. She couldn't not look away or close her eyes at this point because she needed to see what those wild eyes were going to do next.

Djet sunk to his knees and lifted her jade beaded light linen white gown to reveal her ankles first, then he slid the soft fabric up her calves and thighs until the junction between her thighs was inches from his lips.

"I want to fill you with ecstasy, my sweetness."

His hot breath heated her center. The sensation shot through her body, making her breath hitch and her knees buckle. Before she could ready herself, his mouth was over her inner lips, licking, circling, sucking, and biting her essence. He did all of this as his wicked, wild eyes bore into her very soul, leaving her more naked than she initially was, baring the true heart of her femininity in front of him.

Aset never thought sex was this intimate. Lilith always told her it was a necessary evil in life. Sex helped a man relax after a long day of hunting. But this? This was different, and oh, was it so pleasurable for her. She didn't view it as the burden that Lilith had. And if this was what she was in store for every evening, she was all for it, especially if she got to pleasure him as much as he was pleasuring her.

The deliciously devilish tongue built up a pressure with her she'd never felt before. It had her tangling her fingers in Djet's luscious dark locks and guiding his face closer to her just as her back arched, giving him better access to every inch of her. He plunged first one finger inside of her, followed by another after she let out a soft moan of approval.

"You taste divine, my love. Like a honeyed fig, and I need to worship you like the goddess you are."

He continued to plunge his fingers in and out of her center as his tongue circled her bud and she found herself flying over the edge into complete rapture. She dug her nails into his shoulders just as her inner folds pulsated quickly around his fingers. In between hitches of breath, she called out his name as if it were a prayer.

"You are beautiful when you come."

They gazed into each other's eyes for long seconds before he smoothed out her dress and pulled her into his arms.

"Stay with me tonight, sweetness. I need you in my arms."

She tightened her grip on him before she nodded her answer—too spent from the pleasure he'd given her.

"Go to my bed chambers and have Keket prepare a warm bath for each of us. I know you want to keep the rumors down to a dull roar, so make sure Keket prepares both pools. This way, you will have your own. Oh! And have her bring us some wine as well."

"Kama tatamanaa. She said with a smile. "As you wish, my love."

Aset always hated that Yudi chose Adam for the gift of omnipresence and not Lilith. Sure, Aset was there to help nurture the babes to give Lilith a reprieve from the constant caregiving she provided to all of her children and creations, as well as her partner, Adam. But Aset knew she could only do so much.

Aset shot up from her bedchamber as a cold sweat consumed her body. This was the third time she'd seen it in the past couple of nights. The nightmare has different scenarios, but the outcome is always the same. She is facing a demon with her betrothed, Djet, and they die at the hand of their people. This last one, however, was far more bizarre than any other she'd had before within the past seven moons.

Many in her village looked to her as the medicine woman because she had the powers to heal mortals, as well as predict what would happen in the future. She took pride in that. It was the reason they invited her to the court. And once she met Djet's eyes all those weeks ago at the coronation, it was love at first sight for her.

He asked her to dance with him, and after that dance and her vision that ensued after she clasped his hand, the now-appointed king desired her as his sole consort. He not only wanted to predict good fortune as the ruler of Egypt but also for the people of his kingdom as well.

"Why would I address Djet as Raine, and he addresses me as Skye in this new vision? And the clothes? So foreign. It doesn't make much sense."

Aset shook her head to clear the thoughts she'd been verbalizing in the darkness of her bedchamber. Djet had asked her to move into the palace since that first night he'd invited her. Aset was hesitant to accept at first, still worried about his people and the rumors. But once Djet introduced her to his people as their new soon-to-be queen, things changed with the humans. They were kinder towards her, caring even. All of them wanted to get a glimpse of her when she walked by Djet's side in the streets. All of them talked with her in the palace when they'd paid their king a visit. It made her feel good. And perhaps that is why the visions have changed so drastically over the past seven moons. Djet was a famous king. She brushed the covers off her lower body, sighed, and padded across the room.

"I must warn Djet of this vision. Whether the vision made sense to me, it is clear we will battle Demetrese, the ruler of the Underworld, for many, many centuries to come. But first, I must pray to get some clarity."

Aset walked to her altar and lit some herbs. Once

the smoke wafted from the seashell, she placed it next to the clay statue of her beloved goddess, Isis. She then put on a gown for the day and made her way to the throne room. The guards immediately opened the doors to the room as they saw her approach.

"Thank you, Ahmed."

"You're welcome, chantress—uh? I'm sorry! My queen."

She knew the transition was hard on them all. She hadn't married Djet yet, but many of the court and his people bowed and addressed her as if she was their queen.

As the door opened, Djet's eyes brightened.

"My sweetness has brightened my morning! Come, sit next to me and tell me what the goddess Isis whispered to you in your dreams last night."

"I'm afraid the news is not that good, my dearest."

Djet's eyes widened. He squeezed her hand once she approached his throne and placed it in his lap once she sat next to him in her chair. Sure, he'd already had a throne crafted for her even though they wouldn't marry for another few days, but it was because they hadn't married yet that Aset couldn't bring herself to call her chair a throne in the throne room.

"Tell me, my love. What is it? More troubling news about me being usurped?"

"Partly, but that's only half of the vision, I am afraid. I've seen us battle the ruler of the Underworld for the past couple of nights. And not just in this time period. We battle him in others to come. My vision last night was from a modern time—centuries upon centuries from now. I addressed you as Raine in this prophetic dream."

Djet squeezed her hand once more.

"And I call you Skye in that lifetime?"

"Yes?" Aset's eyes widened as she visibly sucked in a breath before continuing. "How did you know?" Her eyes searched his for an answer, but the dark chocolate pools staring back at her gave her little comfort.

"You projected the vision onto me last night, and I saw everything. This isn't the first time I've shared your visions, but it is the first time that they have puzzled me. That is why I asked so quickly about your prophecies. I am connected to you in that way, sweetness, and you know that type of bond is rare in humans, even rarer for us immortals. I believe that is why the goddess Isis herself has blessed this union between us. It is the closest bond any husband and wife will have on earth, and that is why I cannot wait to make you my wife and consort three days from now."

Aset smiled and patted his hand.

"I am glad Isis has blessed me with you as my companion. I couldn't imagine any other life except this one with you. It's as if you and I share each other's breath—not just love. The bond is that great to me."

A heather purple mist began to form in front of them, and suddenly a woman with hazel eyes, pin-straight ebony hair, and a gold crown that resembled a cobra snake appeared before them. Aset and Djet immediately dropped to their knees.

"Rise, my dears. We have much to discuss, starting with the visions I've given you both." She began as she reached out for Djet and Aset's hands.

"Goddess Isis, I didn't expect you to show up unannounced."

"My little sister Aset, my little Nefertiti, I will always come to you if I fear you are in danger."

"So the visions are certain? We will battle Demetrese for centuries to come?" Asked Djet.

"Yes. And I fear the gods will test you in the next few weeks. I believe it was one of them that planted the idea in the ruler of the Underworld's head to go after the both of you. He mustn't win. If he does, good and evil will become unbalanced, and the mortals will suffer for it. We must protect the earth plane at all costs."

"You've shown me that this isn't the only battle, yes. But how is that possible? He's not allowed to walk among the living."

"Yes, that is correct, for the most part. Once a millennium, all the stars and planets align in the sky, making the veil between the Underworld and earth thin. It is because of this he can walk among the living. And if he succeeds, I am worried he will defeat you both."

"But we are immortal. It's impossible for him to kill us." Asked Djet.

"That part isn't clear to me just yet. Other factors are involved." Said Isis.

"Factors?"

"Yes, my sweet Aset. Other factors like Lilith."

"Lilith? What does she have to do with it?" Asked Djet.

"For several centuries, she had been unhappy with Adam and left him, as you both know. However, Yudi suggested she help Demetrese. He's in charge of creating Underworld realms, and she's been creating planes of existence. She's been in the Underworld ever since Yudi banished her from Eden. When she ran from the Garden of Eden, Yudi discovered Lilith was a goddess herself. It was at that point that Yudi, myself, and the other gods and goddesses decided she should go to the Underworld. We feared there'd be an unbalanced power struggle on earth because the only immortals allowed on earth were witches. Since you are not gods or goddesses because we created you to protect the humans on the earth realm, the balance of power remains intact, so to speak."

"I've heard she left him because he didn't believe

they were equal partners. Adam wanted her to submit to him."

"That is correct, Aset. And that is why I've blessed the union between you both. You are each other's equals. You've never swayed. Both of you always think of the other before you make any decisions. That is a very rare gift to share with one another, indeed." Said Isis with a smile that brightened her eyes.

Aset smiled.

"So, why are you worried? Lilith has never been a threat to us. In fact, she's always been the witches' ally." Said Djet.

"And she always will be! Especially with the two of you, of course. You were the first magical beings to help her with her children. She will always protect you from Yudi's wrath."

"Yes, I remember that well, Isis. We enjoyed each other's company while in Eden for that time." Said Djet.

"Hence the special bond. But if Lilith leaves Demetrese, I am afraid of what Demetrese and Yudi might do to the two of you."

"But, again, we are immortal. How can they hurt us?" Asked Djet.

"Demetrese has the ability to create like a god. That means he also has the power to destroy. He can send you into the abyss, and you will not only no longer exist. Your witch powers will then go to the nearest unknowing mortal. We cannot allow a mortal to gain immortal powers because their DNA couldn't handle such power."

"And it would throw off the balance of good and evil."

"Yes, Aset, it would. Demetrese must not succeed under any circumstances."

"We will do our best to serve you, as always, goddess Isis."

"Thank you, Djet. I know you will, but in the meantime, I suggest that both of you train for this battle. You'll need your thermodynamic and energy conversion spells to be perfect."

"I was going to suggest that to Aset once you'd left."

"Very good. I will leave you to your training."

Isis waved a hand in front of them, and the heather-purple mist rose around her feet and then dissipated as quickly from their sight.

CHAPTER FIVE

"I'm scared, Djet."

Djet wrapped his arm around Aset and pulled her to his chest.

"Isis wouldn't have come to us if there wasn't a way out of this mess. The goddess may be many things, but being cryptic isn't one of them."

"We can't tempt fate. She told us there was a possibility we might fail! I can't lose you, Djet. You are my forever love. I couldn't live in a world or a plane where you no longer exist."

Djet cupped her cheek before resting his forehead on hers. He took in a deep breath before continuing.

"Sweetness, you are my forever love as well, and I'm confident we can defeat Demetrese, should it come to that." He gave her a peck on the lips before pulling away. His dark eyes studied her. It was almost as if he was committing each freckle, each laugh line, and dimple on her face to memory. Burning and searing it into his brain as he told her they'd be successful, but Aset wasn't so sure.

One comfort Aset always took was the fact that Djet exuded confidence. Men had that gift, and she welcomed whatever confidence radiated off of him and tried to soak up that energy into herself. She wished she was as confident about the battle ahead, but because Aset was psychic, she saw countless possibilities and outcomes of their future. None of them were good.

A knock on the doors broke her train of thought.

"Sire, someone is here to see you. He says it's urgent. His name is Zhang."

"Send him in, Amon."

Amon stepped aside to allow an older man with salt-and-pepper hair and a beard to match into the throne room. Aset's eyes widened. She recognized the man from her prophetic dreams. Instinctively, she reached for Djet's hand and sucked in a breath. Djet gazed into her eyes and quickly gave her hand a reassuring squeeze after realizing the look of terror that was most likely written all over her face. Sure, she tried to hide it, but she always failed to do so in front of him. He was the only person in existence that could break down her barriers.

Zhang instantly fell to his knees before speaking.

"Sire, I've come to share some disturbing news. I

realize you have a seer, and I mean no disrespect to the chantress and queen, but if my prophetic dream has any truth to it, I feel it is my duty to warn you both."

"You are the one I've seen in my psychic visions! You are the one who may be responsible for our demise!"

"So you've seen these horrid visions that keep me up at night too, my queen?"

"They've been plaguing me for many moons. Tell me, have you seen any other possibilities where we defeat Demetrese?"

"There is one, but I pray it doesn't come to that."

Zhang's eyes lowered to the ground as he stood.

"What do you mean?"

"I may have to become a sorcerer in order to put Demetrese back where he belongs, and I don't like that one bit."

"Well, that's a good thing—isn't it? See, Aset? We can beat the ruler of the Underworld."

Aset gave Djet a small smile. She wasn't sure about any of this, especially when the man before them was haunting her dreams and not in a good way. Still, a warmth washed over her as Djet squeezed her hand and gave her a smile that reached his eyes. Since he was just as intuitive as she was—if not more—she wasn't going to let her fears get the best of her.

"I sure hope that will be the case, your highness.

But I warn you to keep the focus on your spell castings. They will prove beneficial in this fight."

"What if that isn't enough?" She didn't want to ask the question, but there it was, leaving her lips and hanging in the air between them all.

"Then I will become a sorcerer and use all of my powers to resurrect both of you, my queen."

A calmness washed over her once more, and it was at that point that Aset realized she no longer feared the man before her. In fact, she trusted him.

The man pulled something from his long brown robe.

"I've brought a gift to the queen. These are herbs I use for spirit walks. You must burn them and smudge yourself with the smoke in order for it to work. Perhaps this will help you to have visions during the day instead of being plagued with them at night."

A small and easy smile graced Aset's lips. She'd been struggling for a week with fatigue, and now? Now she'd use the herbs so her body could have some well-deserved respite.

"Thank you, Zhang. I will put these to good use."

"I have plenty more growing in my garden. Don't hesitate to ask for more should you need it."

CHAPTER SIX

Demetrese watched as he saw the two of them feeding each other grapes.

"Just look at them. So in love and so made for each other! Why can't Lilith and I be like that? Yudi literally sent her to me, and everything was going so well until it wasn't."

He shook his head and looked at Djet and Aset once more. She was cupping his cheek and laughing at something he was saying.

"This is sheer torture to watch the two of them. Clearly, they have something special and so much so that Yudi has allowed them to live topside on the earth's realm. Why can they do that, and I'm stuck in the shadows, disconnected from everything I've created in the other realms besides the Underworld?"

Demetrese let out a breath and ran a hand down

his face before heading back toward the Underworld in search of Lilith. She'd been away for a full day now, and that wasn't a good sign. The last time she'd run away, she had left Adam. Sure, her version of the story was that Adam was the one that left her, but with each fight they had, Demetrese was wondering just how much of what she'd said was what happened and what parts were her truth and her truth alone.

There were always three sides to a story, and Demetrese knew that better than anyone. There was Yudi's version of kicking Demetrese out of the heavens, his version, and what everyone else witnessed. Demetrese prided himself on having his own version of events as close to the truth others had seen. The only difference was that he'd guarded his heart then. Of course, now wasn't all that different.

He started walking through the planes of existence that Lilith had created when he stumbled upon her with a man. He had long, pin-straight ebony hair, dark eyes that turned red when they mingled with the moonlight, and sharp fangs that replaced normal incisors the minute they set foot on the earth plane. She was gorgeous, strong, and powerful in his eyes. Her appearance mattered little to him, but the moon cast a magnificence on her that he'd never seen before. Demetrese hid in the shadows once more, desperate to find some clarity about Lilith.

She was talking with him in hushed tones, and Demetrese had to strain a bit to hear the gist of the conversation.

"This is a beautiful plane of existence. Thank you for creating it for my children of the night and me."

"Of course! We need to give you a name, however. What would you like to be called?"

"Dracula. It's a fitting name for me."

"Well, you certainly are a handsome devil, and yes, it is fitting, but can I call you Drake?"

"Yes, my queen. You can call me Drake, but that name is exclusively for you alone."

Demetrese sucked in a breath.

Does she like him? Or is he simply one of her creations?

Demetrese inched closer to the couple, hoping to understand.

"Why, Drake, that's sweet of you."

"I'd do anything to please my queen," Dracula said as he cupped Lilith's cheek and brushed it with his thumb.

Lilith placed a palm on his chest and gently pushed him away from her.

"Easy there, tiger. This is getting a little too intimate for my liking."

Dracula let out an exaggerated breath.

"Right. Less intimate. I get it. You want to keep

this platonic because of the ruler of the Underworld."

"Drake, Yudi promised me to him. It's complicated, and so is this." She said as she motioned a hand between the two of them.

"What's so complicated? I like you. You like me. Darling, this all seems pretty simple to me."

"But not to me because I do like Demetrese. I'm just not sure if I like, like him. Hence the complication. If anything, I'm the one making things complicated."

"I can't pretend to understand your situation. Yudi asked you to be Adam's mate, and that didn't work out for obvious reasons."

"Well, yeah! He wants a lapdog—not an equal."

"So what about Demetrese?"

"Demetrese is the perfect gentleman. There's nothing wrong with him. He treats me the way I enjoy being treated."

"I feel the word, but coming on."

"There's no spark. I'm not attracted to him the way I was to Adam."

"Perhaps it's because Yudi literally made you for Adam? Maybe it takes time to develop a spark otherwise?"

"If that was the case, then explain this." She gestured a hand between the two of them once more.

"You made me, Lilith. The answer you seek

should be pretty obvious. I attract you because you made me into something you fancy."

"Well, when you put it that way, it sounds weird!"

"And... Complicated?" Dracula said as he laughed.

Lilith bit her bottom lip.

"Perhaps."

Dracula palmed her shoulders.

"Darling, I can't—no, scratch that. I won't tell you what to do. But I'm going to offer you some advice. Go to Demetrese. Tell him what you are feeling. See if a spark develops. You owe it to yourself and to him."

Lilith let out a breath.

"You're right. You are so right. I need to. Will you forgive me for leaving you here while I sort it out?"

"Of course, darling! You need to figure this out for yourself. I'll be here no matter what you decide."

DEMETRESE LET OUT a breath that he didn't realize he had been holding in, and then he allowed a smile to come over his face. She wasn't exactly head over heels in love with him, but at least willing to give things another go, and that made this shit show before him worth watching. He had to admit; he wasn't a great fan of this Dracula that Lilith had created, but at least the chap—or whatever type of creature he was, had the decency to tell her to come back to him. Of course, if he was in the man's shoes, he probably would say something similar to Lilith, a woman Demetrese quickly grew to realize was more fickle than the wind on the earth realm.

He stayed crouched in his position in the shadows until she left Dracula, and then he sprinted back to the Underworld and took refuge by the river they'd shared intimate dinners on the past few dates he'd had with her. As he snapped his fingers, a table, chairs, grapes, wine, and cheeses appeared. He'd hoped this setting would be pleasing to her, but he couldn't help but wonder if he was making a mistake. The last two dates didn't exactly leave her with a spark, so doing the same thing might be insane. He started to rack his brain for something different, and then she appeared.

Fuck!

It was too late, and he knew it.

"Sweetheart! You are back!"

Lilith smiled, but the smile didn't exactly reach her eyes. He assumed it was because she appeared nervous about her talk with Dracula. He wondered if that was what seemed to be on her mind or if his boring choice in planning a date was.

"I thought you might be hungry, so I whipped us

up some snacks and wine, but if you'd rather do something else, we can."

"No, no. This is fine!"

His lips thinned at the comment she'd made. He couldn't help it. Fine wasn't precisely what he was going for. He needed to impress her because he assumed he hadn't made much headway with her yet.

"Lilith, please talk to me. I've planned our past two dates, and the conversation seemed flat. Clearly, I'm not doing what you like. How about you plan tonight?" He said as he inched closer to her before continuing. "Anything you like! I want to get to know Lilith."

"Okay? Well? If I'm honest, I like the dinners, but they are intimidating."

"Is that why your conversations seem forced to me?"

"Perhaps? I mean—don't get me wrong! These past couple of dates proved to be nice. Intimate. But I also want to have some fun."

"So, what is fun for Lilith?"

"Would you like to go for a swim?"

"Sure. I'll create some clothes for us to wear while we swim in the lake."

"We don't need to create swimwear."

"Why not? Wouldn't that make you more comfortable?"

Before he even finished the sentence, Lilith

stripped herself of her long dress. As it pooled around her ankles, Demetrese drank every inch of her in, from her shapely breasts that boasted rosy pink highlights to her curvy hips, thighs, and calves. And he refused to forget the junction between her thighs that also boasted a rosy pinkness as exquisite as her breasts. Her inner lips were beyond heaven, and he wanted nothing more than to lick every umber colored part of her skin that formed a curve, right along with her contrasting pink features. She was a tall drink in and of herself, something he wanted to drown himself in, and to look at her now with her hooded gaze—all on display for him? Well, that was sheer perfection in his book.

She closed the distance between them, and Demetrese sensed his mouth had gone dry as she sauntered over. Hips swinging oh so seductively and all on display just for him, his mind raced. Why the sudden 180? Why had she been so, for lack of a better term, hell-bent on seducing him?

"It appears you have me at a disadvantage." She said as he swallowed. Hard. And she watched his Adam's apple work, which made him even more uncomfortable.

"Why is that?" His voice shot up higher than he liked.

"Because you have too many clothes on. We need to remedy that if we are to go for a swim together."

He found himself swallowing hard again because his throat felt like he'd been drinking in the desert sand for the better part of the day. Parched from his nerves and parched from a longing for her. An urge to have her in his arms where he knew she should be.

She'd already palmed the hem of his shirt and flung it over his chest before he even registered what to say to her. This strange and deft move on her part seemed something he didn't—scratch that couldn't take in yet. What was she doing to him? Better yet—what was she doing, period? He understood Adam fucked her over, and he promised himself and Yudi that he wouldn't be the guy that Adam had been to her. But now? As she pulled his pants down, a clever combo of the earthly Egyptian linen, he'd grown fond of around his—because hey—maybe now she was going too fast.

His mind went south as he thought of the thin white fabric she'd just divested from her own body. It displayed the rosy pink of Lilith's chest rather well. This was why he'd grown fond of a thicker fabric. He knew this would one day be called jean fabric on earth. He invented it because he thought it to be the best fabric to allow him less temptation with her. His manhood didn't rub up against her so easily, and that was a bonus as far as he was concerned. It didn't allow for as much temptation—or so he thought.

But now? Now as she was divesting him of every barrier he'd created as a wall between them? He was wondering if he'd made a mistake. Perhaps he'd misread her all along? Maybe she really does like him? But then, why talk with Dracula and explain the lack of spark between her and him? Nothing was making sense, and he needed—scratch that—wanted to put some distance between them so he could think.

"Come swim with me!" She said to him as she jumped in and coaxed him with a crook of her index finger.

Usually, for Demetrese, it wouldn't take much to engage in sex. But he hadn't been there with her yet. He wanted to give her time to understand her place in the Underworld. He wanted her to understand him and just how far he'd go to make her comfortable. To make her feel as if she were his equal.

But now? Her eyes were so seductive. Little damned slits as she panted when he walked to meet her in the water. He wasn't sure if he should, but he wrapped an arm around her anyway at her waist. Pulled her close to his rising member, which kept twitching for her. Wanting her. Only her.

Shit!

What was he going to do if she left him for Dracula? It was kinda clear she might if he didn't blow his wad right now. But what he felt for her was more than what she was angling for at this moment.

"I feel something for you I've never felt for any other, Lilith."

His gaze pinned to hers. And he meant it. But if she was still willy wallowing, he wasn't sure if he should press further with her. She had to meet him halfway if this was ever going to work.

She let out a breath. It wasn't something he wanted to hear from her.

"Make love to me—please?"

"What? Are you serious, Lilith?"

"Yes."

She was there. Right there for him. Pliable. But, yeah. He winced. Biting his lip in front of her.

"No."

She let out a whimper.

Fuck! What did I just do?

It was a fucking whimper!

He palmed her shoulder in the lake's drink and began talking before he even realized it.

"I was there when you were talking to your Drake."

Her round pupils went to slits in an almost instant.

"What the fuck? Were you following me?"

"No!"

He swallowed again, knowing he was lying, but couldn't help himself.

"I was walking around surveying my handy work with my realms, and I got lost—I swear!"

She sucked in a breath before responding.

"Okay. I believe you. But we should talk about this."

"Yes, we should. First off, why are you trying so hard? You didn't need to do all of this. I find you very attractive."

Lilith lowered her head before responding.

"I was trying to create that spark. You understand what I mean—don't you?"

"I do, Lilith, but don't you think it would be best if we develop our relationship slowly? It's why I haven't had sex with you yet. I wanted you to feel comfortable with me first. Sexual chemistry, or spark, as you've put it, can come later, my darling."

"Do you think Dracula was right?"

"About?"

"That the spark only happens between the creator and the created."

She wasn't looking at him at this point, and he didn't like that one bit. He raised her chin with his index and forefinger.

"Baby, I told you before. I want you looking at me when we talk. We are equals, and nothing you say to me will make me angry or ashamed of you."

"Are you sure of that? I mean, you caught me with—"

He squeezed her shoulder with his free hand.

"Stop such silly talk. I expect nothing from you, Lilith. You were brought to the Underworld because

Adam broke up with you—and for no good reason, I might add! I don't expect you to blindly take me as yours straight away. You've been hurt, and you need time to heal. Time to think. Don't worry about me and my feelings. I'm doing just fine."

He pulled her into his arms and kissed the top of her head. He was right. The last thing she needed was to have sex. Her mind was scattered at best. Her heart? Probably shattered. And damn it! He wouldn't contribute to the mess.

"Come with me. Let's get out of the water, dry off, and cuddle by the fireplace with your favorite wine."

"Okay."

Lilith immediately crossed her arms over her chest once it was visible outside the water. Yet another sign that sex wasn't a good idea, and he was glad he'd put the breaks on when he did. Demtrese quickly reached for his shirt and put it over her torso before she could protest. Reaching for his pants, he pulled them on and then gathered the rest of their clothing in his hands. He bunched the clothes up in one arm and placed his free palm on the small of her back, guiding her back to his place, a dwelling he hoped she'd one day consider her own one day.

Once they entered his place, he headed straight for his built-in wine cellar just to the right of the breakfast bar. He plucked out a bottle of Bordeaux from the middle shelf and walked to his kitchen

The more he talked with Lilith—the more he got to know her. Well, it was obvious she'd been dealing with the same shit as he was with his father. But she was vulnerable, and to tell her all of this now? That might destroy her. No. He had to keep the terrifying fact that he was Yudi's son from her. Because if she knew that, he knew he'd lose her not only to the bond they seemed to strengthen now with his patience with her but also to the deception of him keeping this vital information from her.

She was clear to him from the beginning that she didn't want an ally because of their commiserating misery with Yudi. It made sense, then. Sense enough that he didn't want it either. At least at the time. His head was so clouded back then. He still hated his father for casting him out of heaven. Sure, his father said it was because he was special—deemed for better things in the Underworld. But Demetrese knew better. His father saw how he didn't get along with any other angel up there. And he wouldn't! Not one of them was created with a stinking backbone like he was!

Hell!

If he didn't know any better, he'd assume his father was creating beings that actually liked and adored him—rather than ones with free will. It made sense, given what Demetrese could do in the Underworld. he could create anything. Any being he saw fit. It could be an obedient minion or a creature hell, especially after Yudi cast him into the Underworld. All alone in a place, Yudi had forced him to create. Sure, the power of creation was nice. But it wasn't what kept him warm at night.

All that power was at his disposal, and nothing made his heart stir until his father practically handed Lilith to him. Sure, it was her last option—his father made that clear to him. Told him that if he couldn't tame her, she'd be recycled into the great abyss. But who was his father to say whose life ends? Yeah, she defied Adam every chance she got, just like she'd been defying him. But? And this was a big but! She did it in a completely loving matter. She wanted nothing more than to better the relationship she'd been cultivating between them. He could only assume she'd done the same for Adam, and that ass let the best thing in his life slip through his fingers. Demetrese wanted to pummel him for it, but if he was really honest? Honest to a fault with himself? He was happy that Adam let her go because now she was with him! And he couldn't be more satisfied with the outcome.

She'd pulled away now, and Demetrese let a whimper escape his lips, mourning for the heat that she contained within her to make him reel with culpability. She was just as guilty as he was in his father's eyes. Yet? All he wanted was to wrap his arms around her and shield her from his father's ridiculous wrath.

seemed to have a mind of its own. But before he could tamp down the rising temperature south of his waistband, she was wrapping her arms around him and pressing her molten hot femininity right up against the tip of his member. It was at that point a moan escaped his lips. He didn't mean for it to happen, but it did, and she met his cry by crashing her lips onto his.

The kiss was explosive, causing tiny currents of electric heat to course throughout his body. She was relentlessly parting his lips at the seam and tangling her tongue with his in a delicious deluge of the taste of her and the Bordeaux they'd been drinking. His hand cupped the nape of her neck, his fingers playing with the mountains of silky pin-straight locks she had. And for a moment—just one solitary moment—he allowed himself to indulge in her. All of her. All that she was giving him.

A pang tugged at his chest, encasing the one part of him that he held dear. That one part he promised himself he'd always guard after his father cast him out of the only heaven he'd ever known. Who does that to a son that merely disagrees with you? Well, his father did. It was a mistake back then to let anyone into his sacred space, and it sure as hell was a mistake now.

Hell...

He'd never pondered the actual word until now. But he sure assumed that the Underworld was his island, where he pulled out one drawer and fished out the bottle opener. He then turned around and opened a cabinet, and pulled out two wine goblets. Demetrese poured a glass and handed it to Lilith before pouring one of his own.

"I don't know what came over me." She said, staring into her wineglass.

"Lilith, please don't worry about it."

"But I do! How could I've acted so—so?"

She let out a sigh before taking a sip of her wine.

"You were acting normal. You only wanted to see if there was a spark. I understand that. But how about we take things a little slower? Maybe let's get the first kiss under our belt before we jump each other's bones."

"See! I was acting silly! You just admitted it."

"No." His voice was softer than he thought it would be. Softer than he wanted to reveal to her right now. "I admit nothing because there is nothing to admit. You need time to heal, Lilith. And I'll be here when you are ready."

Lilith palmed her heart as her eyes welled with tears.

"Demetrese, if I fall, be ready to catch me. Because right now? That's the sweetest thing anyone has ever said to me, and I love you for it."

She crashed into him, her breasts crushed against his chest, making him hard. He chewed the inside of his lip to get a handle on the thing that

that only cared for itself. It didn't matter just as long as it stayed in the Underworld.

Demetrese let out a sigh.

What the hell am I going to do? Because right now, I'm damned if I do, and I'm damned if I don't with this woman.

He hated to admit that to himself because he knew he was right on so many different levels. But damn it! Why'd he have to be right? It wasn't fair.

She was coaxing his lips open again with her tongue, and it was another delicious combination of tasting her and the wine. And—pardon the stupid dad reference—but god, how he loved that taste!

CHAPTER
SEVEN

"I'm afraid!"

"It's understandable, given what you've seen and known."

"I'm not that great at predicting the future, Djet! But I know I can't lose you. I can't live in a world without you in it."

She cupped his face with her palm, and once he settled into her palm, her heart shattered. This man was everything to her. They'd been joined at the hip since Yudi breathed immortal life into them. Their sole purpose was to watch and guard over the humans that Lilith and Adam had. That was it.

To make her live on without her soulmate? This was a huge ask even for a god, as far as she was concerned, because now? Yudi seemed to be fucking them over. At least according to the goddess Isis. Aset hated where this was going. She felt trapped as her nights were consumed with every possibility that might happen to them should they battle Demetrese.

Every. Stinking. Time. They lose the battle. She hadn't seen one positive outcome, and it killed her every damned morning when she woke up with bad news to report to Djet. She didn't see an out in this for either of them, and it wasn't fair. Yudi separated them for so long. And now that after finally being able to be together again, Yudi was making this happen to them. How dare he!

After all? What was he to them? He was a god—sure! But they were immortal witches. Why was he placing blame on them, punishing them? They did no wrong. Even with her mother's—shall she say—indiscretions, which, in all honesty, weren't indiscretions at all. They were simple reactions to what Adam did to her. Still, Aset did what she was supposed to. So did Djet. Why did she have to lose out on happiness just because her mother supposedly screwed up her own chances by questioning a god?

Aset shook her head. The thoughts were utterly absurd. Her mother wasn't any more of a screw-up than she was. Her mother was just a female like her, and Yudi seemed to favor the males in all of his scenarios—at least from what Aset's seen. And to push that now? And this late in the game? It's suicide for them all, including their new ally Zhang.

Too many countless times she saw Zhang's death, and she didn't want that happening either, especially since the human being had been so kind as to help them train for this battle. What was she going to do otherwise? She needed the human alive. There were no reasons to involve humans in a god-slash-immortal war. Which, if she was honest with herself, was happening.

What the fuck did Yudi think would happen with this? Clearly, he wasn't thinking any of this through. They were witches and immortal for a reason! They were supposed to make sure humans discovered no other plane of existence. So if they die? What does that mean for humans? For her proverbial brothers and sisters that her surrogate mother Lilith created? And for all other creatures made in the different planes of existence?

Aset let out a breath that she didn't realize she was holding in, and Djet cupped her face.

"I know all of this is grim, sweetness."

"I don't! What the fuck is Yudi's problem?"

"He is a god. We should not question." He said to her as his palm cupped her cheek and his thumb swiped at a stray tear that she was confident wouldn't escape her flooded eyes just seconds before.

"He is an asshole! Yudi doesn't care about our mother—shit! He doesn't care about us! All he cares about is his first damned creation named Adam, who is more conceded than any other being before or after him!"

Djet pressed his forehead to hers.

"Baby..." His voice broke. Lost in a gasp of breath before he continued. "You can't mean that you want to kill Yudi? He's our god of creation!"

"No! I'd never stoop to such a level! He's almost already gone there, casting so many of us out of Eden like we were criminals. All I want is a balance, something between him and us."

His hand strayed and wandered from her hip up to her breast, coyly playing with the nipple underneath three layers of fabric.

A moan she didn't realize was coming until the electric heat came over her and escaped her lips.

"Djet—we shouldn't. We aren't married yet!"

"And yet? You have predicted our demise before we can even experiment with such bliss with one another. But baby? If Yudi doesn't allow this union?"

His voice stopped short as he licked his lips and then thinned them. She saw the hard swallow as his —truth be told, cliche—Adam's apple was prominent with that swallow.

What the fuck was Yudi doing to her? Killing her? Shattering her into so many infinite pieces that each shard felt like it cut a new part of her skin on her body. Pick a place, and that hurt was there. Deep. To the, for lack of a better term—god damned core!

And maybe that was fitting. Well? Perhaps! Because why? Well, Yudi fucking sucked! And at this point, since she's seen monkeys in the earth realm, that was all she could compare the ass to! So yes, Yudi sucked monkey balls. He was someone who tried to exude great power. But in the end, he was nothing more than an ass-strutting, unworthy god with no chance of having a companion of his own.

If he created his own companion, we all wouldn't have to suffer his insolence! The god clearly wasn't an immortal or a man who was capable of change. Clearly, this was a flaw in him as a god of us all, and Aset knew she had to change that about him, or the entire universe being created would crumble.

Djet's lips grazed her throat now. And with all of her strength, she wanted to put distance between them. To make sure their vows were pure. But with the battle coming and her nightmares, she realized what she wanted most in this world was to have Djet in her arms. So really? How can she say no? How can she deny the only person in her life that makes it easier to breathe? The fact is, she can't. Scratch that. She won't deny her love tonight or any other night for the rest of their lives together. And sadly, that may come true far too soon. Sure, the dreams plagued her with every relentless possibility of her losing him, Raine losing her—which she'd never accept, or them losing each other. But she refused to give up hope. She'd wield that sucker like it was her best weapon until her last breath.

"I don't care what Yudi thinks. All I want is for you to make love to me, Djet. Right now. Please?"

His pupils became huge black pearls within seconds as he tugged at her waist a little tighter before swooping Aset into his arms. Sure, they hadn't been wed yet. And sure, they wouldn't before Demetrese came to delve out their demise of his choosing. She shouldn't give of herself so freely to Raine. The gods wouldn't take kindly to this. They'd pay the price for their disobedience. However, right now? She couldn't—wouldn't think of that, especially since her gods put her in this impossible decision, to begin with. No. Free will had to happen.

"Come with me to my bed chambers, Aset."

"I will."

As soon as they reached his room, he placed her back on her feet, and his lips crashed against hers. Without breaking his kiss, he'd guided her to the bed. Once Aset's calves met the bed, he began divesting her of her dress, jewels, and shoes before removing his own clothing and gently placing her on the bed.

He straddled her, placing a knee around each of her thighs.

"You are so beautiful, Aset." He said as he ran a finger down her face, neck, and chest. Resting it just above the top of her left breast. "These are perfect to look at," He continued as his finger swirled over the nipple of her breast, making it pebble, "but I'd much rather have a taste. I've been dying to know if your essence is as sweet as your day lily perfume."

He trailed kisses from her lips down her jaw, collarbone, and the top of her breast before taking her into his mouth and swirling his tongue around her nipple. A moan escaped her lips as he gave it a nip.

"That's it, sweetness. Enjoy this. Enjoy our love."

He trailed kisses down her stomach until he stopped just below her navel. He pressed a finger inside her inner lips. She gasped, making him press a second, followed by a third, into her slicken walls.

"I can tell you are ready for me, but I haven't gotten my fill of you yet. I still need to drink you in."

His tongue swirled around the top of her entrance before he placed his mouth over it, licking, sucking, and nibbling her until her free hand fisted her hair and her back arched and bucked against his wicked mouth.

"That's it, baby. Come for me."

"Djet, please. Please!"

Her words, both broken and breathy, seemed to sound more like a plea rather than a goddess's demand. Sure, they were both technically demigods. Infused with the blood of their creator and the promise of Lilith's blood surging through them both. Though Lilith never performed a ceremony outright, she didn't need to. Her unconditional love infused the tie between them all.

And it was that bond that could—scratch that! No! It would! Save them all. Aset was determined to make it so.

"Of course. As you wish, sweetness."

He plunged himself inside her, and he began to rock his hips until the both of them bucked and thrust against each other in what could only be deemed as a twin-like motion. This was the first of its kind in existence, and Aset could feel the sting of Yudi as the heat between them set them ablaze. Aset may not be a pure warrior goddess, but she had an arsenal all of her own, and she planned to use it against Yudi and Demetrese.

As moans escaped both of their lips, a pool of pleasure jetted deep inside her. She cupped his backside in a desperate attempt to hold on to the last ripple in their wave of passion—something she'd been doing in the past days. She needed to savor every last bit of love from him—just in case. Once the last of his seed coursed through her, he collapsed on top of her in a tangled mess of arms and legs.

"I love you, Djet."

"And I love you, princess."

CHAPTER
EIGHT

They weren't getting much closer, and Demetrese knew their relationship had died. She never tried to kiss or make love to him after her last effort, which was weeks ago. And, of course, he had no one to blame but himself for that. Stupid him said no because he had morals and principles. Yudi might disagree, but Demetrese did have morals.

What will it take to get through to this woman?

He had to admit this woman drove him crazy. Crazy to the point where he'd fallen in love with her. She was the most beautiful woman he'd ever laid eyes on. And was confident beyond a shadow of a doubt that he was falling unequivocally and irreparably in love with her.

But? None of it mattered because she wasn't in love with him—and not even a little.

Demetrese let out a sigh as he headed to his countertop bar. He poured himself a generous three-fingered shot of bourbon and brought the amber liquid to his lips. He knew said liquid was not filled with enough magic to help him forget his troubles, but the slow burn sure did wonders for dulling the pain. Of course, the dull ache could have stemmed from being numb. Numb to love. Or perhaps it's apathy?

Why was it so easy for some people to fall in love and so damned hard for him? Djet and Aset made it look effortless to open up to each other. Their passion seemed transcendent as they fed one another grapes. Never once taking their eyes off of each other. The adoration they shared seemed to drip off of them, and that love was exuded from all of their people in Egypt as well.

His subjects didn't particularly care for him. Well, that wasn't entirely true. They were grateful to him for creating them, but that's all the love he'd gotten. Gratefulness wasn't much compared to someone doting on you. No one adored him. And all of that reminded him how even his father only tolerated him. Well, if being cast out of heaven and imprisoned in his hell hole is his father's way of tolerating him, then that's what he was to Yudi.

Demetrese hadn't a clue what to do at this point, but he knew he hated the fact that Lilith was putting more distance between them. There was little he could do to change that because she was off to god knows where doing god knows what. He wrapped his hand around the decanter containing his liquid bliss of oblivion, ready to pour another heavy-handed pour when a thought hit him. Why not fight for Lilith's attention? That would show her just how much he loved her. He took the last swig of his drink, placed it on the countertop, and headed out to the planes of existence that Lilith had created.

It wasn't long before he came upon her and her creation, Dracula. A pang of anger rose in his belly as he took refuge in the shadows in an attempt not to disturb them. But as he got closer, his rage erupted into a volcano of emotions because Dracula was touching her the way he'd wanted to touch her all along. Dracula was kissing her soft lips, drinking her in.

What the fuck? She promised him—promised me—that she'd give us a shot, and I see that was all an act?

Demetrese ran back to the Underworld and headed straight for his bourbon. He poured another drink and took a sip to calm his rage. But it was no use. The burn in his throat only seemed to give rise to more madness.

That bitch needs to understand just how much she's hurting me. Wait? Fuck that shit! I wouldn't be dealing with this if Yudi didn't send her down here in the first place. Her dismissive, flaky, fickle behavior has nothing to do with me. Clearly, Adam was onto something when he cast her out of Eden! She's nothing but a harlot, and I'll show her!

His lips curled upright as his mind synced with his gut, erupting a plan as dark as the night.

The only thing that will hurt her the most is if I go after the only thing she cares about—well, the only two things—Djet and Aset! I'll destroy them both!

CHAPTER NINE

"Do you think I'm crazy, Drake?"

"Not at all, my darling. If you say that you are worried about what Demetrese might do, by all means, stay here and contact Djet, Aset, and Isis."

"Isis already knows of my concerns and has warned the two. Still? I'm worried I haven't taught those two enough magic to ward off Demetrese. I wouldn't put it past him to go after them."

"Would you like me to come with you? Just to protect you. Nothing more."

Lilith palmed Dracula's forearm.

"I'd like that very much. Thank you for being here for me. It means a lot to me. Makes me feel like you truly care about me."

"I do care," Dracula said as he wrapped an arm

around her waist and pulled her close. "A lot more than you think. I'm falling in love with you."

Lilith smiled.

"I'm falling in love with you, too. It's just I didn't want to tell you until I broke things off with Demetrese. I mean—technically, there's been nothing there. We've never consummated the relationship. And that's more on my end. I didn't get close to him after I realized my feelings for him only ran as deep as a great fondness. Nothing more."

"I understand, darling. I understand."

"I really don't want to hurt him. He's been so good to me. Well, up until now, of course. I've never seen him this restless, this angry at anything. I'm not sure why he's acting this way."

"Well, let's go warn Djet and Aset. Maybe they have a better understanding as to why Demetrese has been acting the way he's been acting."

"Good idea."

IT DIDN'T TAKE Lilith and Dracula long to get to Egypt and the palace. Surprisingly, they weren't allowed in immediately, which worried Lilith. It was one thing to limit visitors of the human kind—but immortals? It seemed absurd.

The palace guards ushered them to a room with two chairs on a platform. Lilith assumed this was the greeting area for their subjects. She patiently waited for them both to come to her, and it wasn't all that long before they did.

"Lilith! It's so nice to see you!" Aset said as she went over to embrace Lilith. Once she pulled away, her gaze settled on Dracula. "And you are?"

"My name is Dracula."

"I expected your name to be Demetrese." Said Djet.

"It's not, but we have come here to warn you about him."

Aset sucked in a breath as she clasped Lilith's forearms.

"Then it's started? Demetrese plans to kill us?"

The blood drained from Lilith's already pale complexion.

"He plans to kill you? Is that what you've seen in your visions, my dear Aset?"

"Yes."

"Well, surely there's something we can do."

"No, Lilith. I've dreamed of every potential outcome and scenario, and we will both die at Demetrese's hands." Said Aset.

"I won't have this! You are both my everything. You kept me positive and helped me stay strong every day Adam went out hunting. I wouldn't have endured any of it well if not for the two of you."

"Darling, why don't we teach them as much as we can about the dark arts? It might help them stay alive."

"You are right, Drake. That can help."

"It's worth a shot."

The four went to the private chambers of the palace to join Zhang so they could train.

CHAPTER TEN

It had been three long days since he'd caught Lilith with Dracula, and she didn't bother to return. Nor could he find either of them in the planes of existence. He'd tried to calm himself during these last three days, but with each passing morning, he grew angrier and angrier at her for throwing his love away for her.

He'd tried sipping his favorite drink, bourbon, but it didn't give him solace. Festering while waiting for Lilith to decide to grace him with her appearance wasn't helping either. He slammed his drink down on the countertop and headed for the earth plane, where he knew he'd get some solace right along with some revenge.

It wasn't long before he reached the palace and saw Lilith with Dracula, Djet, and Aset. Another man was also with them that Demetrese did not recognize, but it didn't matter. He'd kill all of them if he had the chance. He lunged for Djet, the one with the most power in the room. If Demetrese could kill Djet first, it would be easier to kill the rest of them since he knew all too well that he'd inherit Djet's immortal powers just by killing him.

Demetrese's fist made contact with Djet's jaw. Still, the man Demetrese did not know stepped to the forefront, throwing energy balls at Demetrese. They were strong, but nothing compared to what Demetrese could throw back.

"Is that all you have, old man? I can do better!"

Demetrese concentrated on his outstretched hands and worked his energy between them. A whitish-grey lightning formed into a ball and increased in size, double what the old man had thrown at him moments before. He raised his hands and lunged the ball toward the man.

Right before it reached the man, Lilith stepped in front of it. Demetrese's eyes widen. In all of his rage about Lilith over the past three days, he'd never wanted to direct his anger right at her. He loved her. And at this moment in time, he realized he still loved her and couldn't see her die. He outstretched his hands once more to direct the ball of energy away from Lilith. They locked eyes just as the ball slid to the right of her.

It then made contact with Aset. She locked a gaze onto Djet and let out a whimper.

"I love you, Djet. Never forget that!"

Smoke and a pungent smell of charred flesh instantly filled the room as she fell to the ground. Her body was limp.

"No, no, no, no! Aset!"

Raine ran to Aset's aid, but it was too late. She let out one last breath before a blue light came from her body and shot into Demetrese. A surge of power swept over him. An ability he didn't realize she possessed. He always thought Djet was more powerful than her. And rightly so, Yudi seemed to breathe the power of dominance in all of his male creations. But clearly, Demetrese was wrong. This woman possessed greatness all of her own.

Lilith lunged at Demetrese's chest and beat on it with her fists.

"How could you! How? You knew she and Djet meant the world to me, yet you destroyed her as if she were nothing! I hate you! I. HATE. YOU!"

And there it was, right in front of him, on display. All the disdain and sheer loathing he thought he'd enjoy in Lilith's eyes. But instead of relishing this moment in time, all Demetrese felt was tortured pain. This pain was different, though. It ran more profound than that. Lilith could have kicked him in the balls, and he wouldn't feel more than a dull ache in his nether region. No. This pain, the one that made his insides feel empty, was far worse than any other physical or mental pain he'd gone through since the first day that Yudi breathed life into him.

Djet let out a cry that turned into a growl.

"You bastard! You fucking bastard! She was my queen! My forever! My constant beacon in this horrific hell known as earth, and you—YOU—took her from me! I'll kill you for this! Mark my words." Djet spat the words in rapid-fire succession.

Djet lunged for Demetrese and latched his hands around Demetrese's throat. Demetrese clutched Djet's hands, but as Demetrese suspected, Djet was powerful, and he struggled to break the hold.

When his lungs quit on him to breathe more air, Lilith wrapped a palm around Djet's shoulder.

"Djet, please don't do this. Demetrese is wrong—I know that as well as you, but he shouldn't be killed over this."

"Yes, he should," Djet said, not breaking his icy gaze from Demetrese. "And I want to watch his last breath snuffed out of his lifeless body. Serves him right since he made me see that horrific sight of my love perishing only moments ago."

"But think of what Yudi will do to you! He will recycle you! I can't lose you both. I won't."

"Lilith, my life is worthless without Aset. I'd rather die a thousand deaths than endure another minute without my queen by my side."

"That can be arranged." Said Yudi as he materialized in front of them all. "Let Demetrese go! Final warnlng."

"No. Demetrese must die for his mistake."

"Then you leave me no choice, Djet."

Yudi snapped his fingers, and Djet dropped into a heap on the floor. Lilith dropped in unison in front of Djet.

"Djet? No!"

She shook him at first to wake him, but shortly she pulled him to her chest and wailed, mourning his nonexistence.

Yudi rushed to Demetrese's side, but he, like Lilith, soon realized that Demetrese was just as lifeless as Djet.

"You did this, Lilith! This is all YOUR fault!" Yudi spat as he put three of his fingers together to snap them. "I should have done this a long time ago."

Before he could snap his fingers, Isis appeared before them while Lilith began reciting a spell.

"I am Lilith and made of the dust of the earth. Heed my words, for they are of a hefty girth. You are an angry god who has caused a rift in every plane. And I ask for the power of all that is good to rectify this atrocity, though not in vain. Gods and goddesses from above and below grant me the power to overthrow all that Yudi was and is. So mote it be!"

A dark cloud consumed Lilith just as Yudi snapped his fingers. But Lilith didn't drop to the floor. Instead, her skin became paler to the point she was a grayish-white complexion that closely mirrored Dracula's and Demetrese's. Her incisors lengthened, and her fingernails grew several inches from the regular close-to-tip length she'd had before. Lilith lunged at Yudi and bit the flesh that met Yudi's neck and collarbone.

"Enough!"

Isis appeared next to them all and extended her hand. Gray lightning shot from her index finger, separating Lilith from Yudi.

"The fighting is done! No more shall die by anyone's hands on this day!"

"She is my creation, Isis. By law, I may recycle her as I see fit."

"That was before you allowed your other creations to overthrow the balance of all the planes, Yudi. Do you realize the atrocity you have caused? Lilith has become one of the creations you cast out of Eden and placed in the Underworld! She's now a demon whose sole purpose is to keep you in check! No Yudi. Your authority on this matter is revoked, and you must correct this wrong. You will bring Djet and Aset back to life. They are immortal witches that deserved none of this. Their purpose in life was pure. Not once did they ignore your rules or laws. Right until the end, they were pure of heart."

"But Djet killed Demetrese!"

"Wasn't it you, the ruler who created the word smite, say something like 'an eye for an eye?'"

Yudi nodded.

"I did."

"So again, why did you allow two immortals to be recycled? The law states that power can only be transferred to a human, or the balance of good and evil is jeopardized. Demetrese wasn't a human. Therefore Djet had every right under your law to destroy the fallen angel."

YUDI LET out a sigh before continuing. He hated where this was going, but Isis was right. The balance of power was now askew, and he only had himself to blame. If he'd only come to Demetrese earlier, none of this would have happened. But he trusted Demetrese would have had compassion. He did, but it was all too late for the situation to be rectified.

Still? He could distribute the balance of power fairly and smite Lilith on a completely different level. His gaze met hers. She wasn't looking into his eyes. She withered, drawing in on herself. Her entire being seemed to be catatonic. Yudi liked this Lilith because it was the first time he'd ever seen her pliable, completely and utterly broken, and he had a hand in that. Yudi smiled a small smile, but only to himself. He didn't dare show his minor victory to Isis. The goddess would remove his balls from his inner thighs, fashion them into gold, and bury them somewhere on earth where it would no doubt take him nearly a century or twelve to find. The woman was a bitch in the highest sense. No wonder the god Ra listened to her obediently.

Even still? He wanted to control that smile slapped across her face. It was why he created the earth, to begin with. He wanted men to overcome the constant nagging of having to get permission from their female counterparts. Sure, he didn't have one himself at the moment, but it didn't mean he hadn't had the pleasure of a goddess in his bedchambers. But this? This took things way too far.

"Fine!" He snapped his fingers, and Djet and Aset appeared. "They are now back here and will live the rest of their mortal lives here on earth in Egypt. As mortals, they will live a life susceptible to human demise. And since their previous lives had them living a life of becoming usurped, they will meet that demise again as humans, where they will feel the pain of every death they have in their futures. I, Yudi, god of all creation, will allow humans to repent their mistakes in a new life of their choosing from now until forever and a day. Both Djet and Aset can continue to love each for forever as long as they wish. And in each life, they are born into. However, I grant free will to them and every other human. This means they have to work harder at loving each other by first finding one another on earth and then making sure they want to fall in love again. That is what I say shall be."

"What about the balance of power? Are you forgetting they were immortal?"

"Not at all, Isis."

His fingers snapped again, and a ball of energy rose from them and hit Zhang.

"Now it is up to this sorcerer to maintain the balance of all creatures with powers here on earth. He is my eyes and ears."

Yudi allowed a smile to spread across his lips before he vanished into a clouded mist.

Djet rushed into Aset's arms.

"Baby! I thought I lost you forever."

She kissed his temple.

"Never. You are my forever."

Isis cupped one-half of the couple's shoulders, and Lilith cupped the other half.

"Now that all is righted let's plan the wedding." Said Lilith.

"Yes, let's!" Said Isis. "Earth needs a celebration."

CHAPTER
ELEVEN

EPILOGUE

Yudi returned to the Underworld, a smile still on his lips, as he snapped his fingers.

Demetrese appeared before him.

"What am I doing back here?" Demetrese asked him the moment the fog cleared between them.

"You are doing exactly what I ask of you. From now on, you are the sole ruler of the Underworld, and now? Now you have the power to turn witches into black-hearted ones. You can start with Djet and Aset."

Demetrese smiled a smile that turned into a cackling laugh.

"What do I need to do?"

"First, there are these rings I'd like to gift you.

They pack quite a punch of power. After a witch performs their initiation ceremony, I grant you a full day to turn a good witch into evil."

"Twenty-four hours will be all I'll need."

THE END... FOR NOW...

BEFORE YOU GO...

Did you enjoy Forever Loved? If so, you can sign up for my newsletter where I offer more fun and freebies!

https://www.authoramandakimberley.com/newsletter-signup

IF YOU LIKED FOREVER LOVED YOU MIGHT LIKE...

Midnight & Mistletoe

Midnight Rising Series

USA TODAY BEST SELLING AUTHOR

Amanda Kimberley

MIDNIGHT & MISTLETOE
CHAPTER ONE

Priya tried to braid her hair again for the fourth time, but she still couldn't get the frizz fest to behave itself.

"It's no use. I'm going to have to jump in the shower and drench it."

It was the first day of her new life, and everything had to be perfect since she'd be working with "*the*" Braden Boss, a highly successful chef with his own TV show on The Food Channel. She wasn't horribly keen on having had to use her womanly wiles on the man to get the job, but her daddy always said, 'If you've got it, flaunt it.' And her triple D cup size surely became a definitive flaunting mechanism with this man.

Three years ago, she wouldn't have had to stoop so low to allow her physical features to speak for her successes. Her money and fame in the business world made her a respected woman back then. But now, after everything she'd suffered, including her own dignity ripped from her, she found herself starting over. Sadly, she had less than when she was fresh out of college, which proved to be the worst low of her life. Because now? Now she needed to be content with playing second fiddle as a sous-chef to one of the most famous culinary brilliants in the business today. Not that she couldn't share the spotlight. She was good at that, but given what she knew about Boss, he wouldn't share it—he'd hog it.

The braid finally took shape after she drenched her hair, and she secured it with a hair tie before she let out a tremendous sigh.

"Please, my dear Lord, let me get through today with little to no problems. It will be bad enough to swallow my pride for the next 10 hours because the last thing I need is an ogling boss or a botched dinner."

She put on a little foundation, blush, and

mascara—not wanting to look as if she just came off the runway since what she had on was distracting enough. The man—at least during the interview proved incorrigible, only hiring her for her perky assets, so she didn't need to prove him right by gussying herself up to the nines. He never looked north of her chest during the hour-long interview. That alone convinced her the tabloids had been right. He was a billionaire bad-boy who only had a serious relationship with his coffee maker. Of course, she had something in common with his Keurig. The man knew how to push her buttons.

She grabbed her purse and keys and headed out the door. The drive to The Odd Duck wasn't far from her apartment via the highway. But come winter, she'd have to leave her house two hours early during a snow "storm" to use the back roads if she had any hopes of getting there on time. Southerners weren't exactly known for being able to drive in inclement weather. Two inches of snow here would compare to a blizzard up in New England—at least according to her cousins from New York City. Texas though? They shut everything down because they can't treat the highways with massive car pileups. And she was not looking forward to January and February, which were only a few short weeks away. It was almost unheard of to land a job in the restaurant field so close to the holidays.

Sure, waitstaff positions were always open, but

typically not management. Not that Priya needed the money for Christmas gifts, most of her family was long since buried. Still, since her divorce, she made it a point to look forward to treating herself with a lavish Christmas gift. She felt she deserved it after the hell her ex put her through, and she wasn't going to back down on such a thing this year. It was the first year she could use money from a paycheck instead of her bank account, and she would take pride in herself for accomplishing so much in such little time. She knew no one else at her age that had to start over. Sure, some people go back to school and change careers after retirement, but she was far from her golden years, and she wasn't about to live off her dividends alone. No. She wanted a sense of accomplishment just like anyone else did in their barely thirties did.

She found a parking space a lengthy distance away from the restaurant under a streetlight and pulled in. Once she turned the car off, she let out a long breath to steady her nerves before opening the door. This was like her first job-first day jitters all over again. She slowly placed both feet on the ground and locked her car, trying to stamp out some of her nerves before proceeding toward the entrance. Her stomach did a few backflips as she tried to put one foot in front of the other to make it to the door.

Once through the threshold, a hostess greeted

her. Her eyes were half-mast and sunken in, and the hap-hazard eyeliner she applied appeared as if it was from the night before. The bags under her eyes were the most prominent feature of her pale face. She looked overworked and overloaded. Priya scanned the restaurant to see if the rest of the staff was just as tired and most likely hungover, and to her astonishment, it appeared they all were. This was clearly something she needed to change if the place was ever going to appear upscale and professional. The Odd Duck wasn't a chain restaurant with a revolving door of employees. It was established with the intent of being a leading dining experience from ingredients provided by local farmers.

The minute she knew she was interviewing with Boss, Priya began dreaming about Michelin Stars—not that The Odd Duck was even thinking about upscale. They started out humbly like any other restaurant with an unusual yet awesome goal. They only used ingredients from local farmers so they could provide a local unique experience, something Priya could get behind. Now that he had hired her, she wanted the best recognition she could get for the restaurant and for Brayden. Priya cleared her throat, plastered her biggest Southern smile, and asked where the boss was. The hostess's eyes widened.

"We don't call Mr. Boss 'the boss.'" She said with

air quotes. "He absolutely hates that. Just a fair warning since this is your first day, Ms.?"

"Priya Pant, but please, call me Priya! I'm not one for such formalities among adults I work with." She bounced out the words as she extended her hand to the hostess, whose lips seemed to thin to nonexistence by the minute. The woman, who wasn't much older than Priya, flicked her eyes to the extended hand and then back to Priya's gaze.

"Um, you might want to rethink what you've got going on as a first impression. Because the formality of your name is about the only thing respected around here. Again—fair warning. Come on. I'll show you to the kitchen." She said as she turned on her heel and motioned for Priya to follow.

Priya lowered her hand and frowned. She was barely in the door and was already having one of the worst days of her life.

Who doesn't shake hands? Clearly, none of them here! That needs to change.

Priya sucked in a breath as the hostess opened the door to the kitchen. She then motioned for Priya to walk in. Priya's brow furrowed as the hostess turned to walk away.

"Aren't you going to take me to Mr. Boss?"

"Hell no! I stay as far away from the kitchen as I can. No offense, lady? But good luck to you! Maybe I'll see you outside for a smoke break. We like to have bitch sessions out there. Of course, that's if you survive that long."

Priya narrowed her eyes. "I don't smoke."

The hostess laughed loud and long. It almost sounded like a cackle.

"Well, you may not be a smoker now, but I predict you probably will start up soon! Mr. Boss isn't exactly the easiest person to get along with. I figured I'd give you a fair warning since you didn't figure that out from my candor at the door."

Priya shook her head at the clearly deranged woman. There was little she could do to fix the girl's attitude this early in her sous-chef career at The Odd Duck, but she vowed she'd try. She sucked in a long breath and headed into the kitchen.

A loud clanging filled the air, followed by a mouth so foul she wondered if the vegetables were still fresh.

"Son of a bitch! This sauce tastes like absolute ass! A five-year-old can do better! Make it again, God damn it! And this time—season it before you put that shit in the pan! You graduated from Cornell, for Christ's sake! I expect the best from you, for fuck's sake!"

Priya palmed her reddening cheeks. In all her years of growing up as a minister's daughter, no more than two swear words passed her daddy's lips. And now, her new employer, Braden Boss, said more explicit remarks in two minutes than she had ever heard in her entire lifetime.

Jesus, Mary, and Joseph! What have I gotten myself into?

Braden looked up from the now crying young prep woman and locked his eyes on Priya.

"Thank God you are here! At least someone with an ounce of talent can help me with this fucking train wreck!" He said as he tossed his hands in the air. "Come with me to my office, and we'll go over some itineraries for today's specials. After that, I will have you work with Ms. Fucking Prima Donna right here, so my recipes come out the way I intended them to and not with an added flavor spin that sucks monkey balls. The only way for this restaurant to succeed is for everyone to fucking execute the dishes properly!" He said this in a low growl through gritted teeth before motioning Priya to another area of the kitchen with a door.

Priya stood frozen in her stance. Her knees locked as she tried to will them to move. She did not know that she'd be walking into *Hell's Kitchen* with the Devil reincarnate as her boss, but Priya did get a few things as she was willing her feet to think for themselves. First, she had to force her legs to walk fast because he was already halfway across the kitchen in two strides. Two, she would not give this heathen the satisfaction of watching her burn under the collar. And three, paying for the roof over her head depended on her compromising with this Lucifer. Daddy always taught her about signing her soul away. But clearly, Daddy never met *the* Boss that could accomplish that just by signing her paychecks.

Somehow, somehow, she could put one shaking foot in front of the other and make it to his office.

"Shut the door." He motioned to her as she stepped through it.

He locked on her eyes, but as soon as she sat down in the empty seat opposite him, his eyes went south. Priya frowned at the gesture. Sure, she stooped to a new level of stupid with getting hired, but that didn't mean she had to take his ogling daily at work. He should be more of a professional gentleman, but clearly—he didn't get the memo.

"So, Ms. Perky, let's talk about the specials for today." He said with a smile, eyes still locked on her chest.

Priya bent down slightly in her chair to meet his gaze and waved a hand in front of his eyes.

"Hi. First off, my eyes are north of where you are looking. Second, it's Priya—not perky." She said as she crossed her arms over her chest.

It didn't do much to cover up her enormous triple-D cups, but she certainly didn't want to get the attention she had been in his office for the last few minutes.

He chuckled.

"Whatever you say, Ms. Perky."

Priya let out a huff.

Braden cleared his throat and lowered his gaze to the floor before continuing. "Sorry, Ms. Priya. So, let's get down to business and pick from these four for today's and tomorrow's specials. I was thinking either quail stuffed with fresh figs and prosciutto or quail in rose petal sauce for the first choice and for the second either smoky citrus butter-baked redfish or mustard-maple roasted salmon." He said as he spread some notes onto the desk in front of her. His fingertips brushed her hand slightly as she reached for one page of notes and an electric heat surged through the tips of her fingers that traveled right down to her core.

There was no denying that Braden was attractive with his luscious dark and wavy locks and chestnut brown eyes. His solid forearms and citrus, musky scent drove her to the point of insanity too. But no amount of crazy would be worth an attraction to the foul-mouthed buffoon. She shook her head in protest of her body's reaction and crossed her legs to stop her libido from singing any amount of praise to the gorgeous god before her. He was her employer, and that was that.

"Well, my specialty is Italian and Southern foods. I'd love to work with the prosciutto and fig recipe because it sounds fun and flavorful. As far as the fish goes—wild salmon is in season now through August, so we should take advantage of the mustard-maple recipe. Even the maple syrup will be delicious now because it is also in season. The redfish recipe sounds mouth-watering, but I'd wait till August for that one. Perhaps we can do smoked citrus for a salmon dish for tomorrow instead?"

Braden smiled from ear to ear. "Apparently, I was right about you being sharp. I threw in the red herring—or in this case—the redfish to see if you knew what was seasonal. I've always found fish should be in season for a perfect meal because it just tastes better." His eyes met hers for the first time since they walked into his office, and she could see they were twinkling with delight as he talked about food. It was the first time he appeared human instead of a horny bastard.

"I know we talked briefly in the interview, but I never got to ask what your favorite dish is to prepare."

He was clearly searching, and Priya was tongue-tied. No man should look that gorgeous! It should be a crime against humanity. Of course, his potty mouth left much to be desired, and she focused on that to get the wheels in her brain to move. Still, what could she possibly say to impress this famous chef?

"Well, in all honesty, it would have to be manicotti." She blurted out the statement almost without thinking it over. She drew out her pronunciation of manicotti in an Italian/New York/Southern drawl. "My grandma made them from scratch every Thanksgiving, and I make them on special occasions in her memory. I do the same with lasagna, too—even though she didn't make that as much."

His eyes brightened again. He got up from behind his desk and reached out to cup Priya's cheeks. Priya shot up from her chair. Sure, she thought the guy was a hornball, but she never thought he'd touch her this brazenly in his own office, at which any point someone could enter. They were nearly a breath apart, and Priya sucked in as much air as she dared through her slightly parted lips. He couldn't know he had this effect on her because she wouldn't allow it.

"Priya, I didn't care about the dish you'd tell me. All I cared about was the passion behind it. I knew my gut was right about hiring you." He said while he pressed his lips on both of her cheeks and made a soft smacking sound. They were so buttery smooth, and she barely realized he was kissing her until he met her gaze again. She tried to recoup her look of horror, but she wasn't doing very well in hiding it. "Sorry! I don't mean to make you uncomfortable. It's just that you remind me of my family. They were all chefs and all from Europe. I'm sure you know it's customary to greet each other by kissing cheeks."

"Really? You didn't care about the dish?" She found her hands cupping both of his that still cradled her face. She blinked a second longer than she needed to as Priya moved into his touch, but only slightly before she corrected herself. *He's your boss, Priya! Stop panting over him!* "And no, the European greeting isn't uncomfortable for me. I'm literally second-gen off of the boat. My grandparents were the first to arrive here off Ellis Island. After growing up in my family and spending a summer abroad, I'm used to the warm welcome in Italy and Spain. My dad's side has been here far longer. He's from India originally." Her eyes widened at her own realization of surprise and shock intermixing her feelings at his gesture. She didn't want such closeness with the man because of who he was, yet her body hummed the instant he touched her.

"Yes, my family is mostly from Europe and mostly Italy, though I have some India descent in my family tree on his side, too." He said as he lowered his hands and placed them in the pockets of his skin-tight black jeans.

God, how she wished to be those hands touching his skin through that thin layer of fabric on his thighs. *Priya! Don't, girl! It's barely an hour into your first day!*

"Sounds nice. Mine were mostly from Italy, too."

"I wish I could have them here for the holidays. Unfortunately, they are all deceased."

"I'm sorry to hear that. It's always hard when our loved ones have passed. I've had my fair share of family members dying these past few years, too. There aren't that many of mine left either. I've got some cousins on my grandfather's brother's side, and that's the side from India. But that's about it."

"Yes, and sadly, you can't do anything except live on without them."

"True." Priya lowered her gaze.

Not knowing what more to say, she quickly changed the subject. This was the first time she met and connected with her boss, and she'd be damned if she screwed this up. She had to get him to like her; talking about dead relatives would not cut it.

"So, have we decided on quail stuffed with prosciutto and figs?"

"I think so. Come back to the kitchen, and I'll show you how I make and plate it." He said as he patted her shoulder and smiled.

Another wave of energy surged through her body as his hand patted her shoulder, and she swore her stomach did a backflip.

They both worked in relative silence in large part in the now all too massive kitchen for the first few minutes as they diced up some onions and garlic. To Priya's surprise, it was an extremely comfortable quiet between them. Usually, when getting to know a coworker, she'd fill the time with idle chat, but this time was different. She didn't feel a need for it. He didn't swear up a firestorm as he had earlier in the morning, which was a welcome relief. But he didn't talk all that much either. However, he did tower over her shoulder as she seasoned the quail with salt and pepper on her cutlery board. She wasn't one to use more than the pinch her ancestors told her to use. Sure, some of them would argue as she grabbed the seasoning between her fingers. But in the end, they all seemed to celebrate once she gingerly salted and peppered her meal. A rush of heat shot through her as he gently tapped her on her forearm.

"Very good. Now rub the meat with this herbal poultry mix and butter like this." The tone was as soft as the touch of his hands over hers.

"Make sure you get every curve—I mean cranny. Rub every part of that thing, so it browns well."

She laughed internally after she let out a shaky breath. Clearly, she wasn't the only one moved by the love they were making in this kitchen.

Priya! Stop it, girl. No sexy thoughts while you make food!

"Yes, sir." She had to say something and thought it was best to jest with a cheeky smile.

"Here," He handed her the figs and prosciutto to place inside the bird's cavity.

His hand grazed hers again, sending another course of electric heat through her arm and traveling straight to her core.

"Thanks." She directed her gaze at the bird in a desperate attempt to avoid eye contact.

"That looks beautiful."

"Thanks. I think it looks good, too."

"The quail?" He whispered in her ear as he bent over her.

"Yes, the quail. What did you think I meant?" She asked as heat rushed to her cheeks when she turned to meet his gaze.

His lips turned into a broad smile.

"I'm asking if you could pass me the quail so I can place it in the oven, but if you must know, that dish isn't the only beautiful thing in this kitchen."

She swallowed hard before handing him the dutch oven that contained the quail, and he placed it in the oven. She quickly busied herself with chopping some lettuce for the side salads they were pairing with the quail.

The aroma of the quail browning beautifully in the oven touched their noses after an hour of baking. Braden pulled them out and smiled as he turned to her.

"Smells and looks like perfection." He said while he made up a plate. "I'll leave you to plating yours as I have shown you here." He said as he started wiping his hands. "You can sample these since this was a practice plate. I'll catch you before the dinner rush. I have a taping to do for the show and will be out for the rest of the afternoon."

Priya smiled at him briefly before getting to work on plating the dish. She watched him leave the kitchen. It was bittersweet to see him go because even though his backside was genuinely exquisite, she had to admit that a part of her wanted him to stay. Cooking up something a little more with her than just a dish was looking to be more on her menu than she cared to admit to herself. And she blushed at the thought of feeling that way about her boss.

Having spent more time with him proved he wasn't as intimidating of a person as she initially thought he was. Still, she was happy that he wouldn't be breathing down her neck for the next few hours, giving her the freedom to walk about the kitchen without brushing against his hard body. The back of her neck began to sweat just thinking about how many times his hips touched hers while chopping away. And the reprieve would give her something else. It would be the chance she needed to build a rapport with the others in the restaurant. Especially that crazy hostess and the poor prep chef who was still sulking in a dark corner of the kitchen.

Priya knew she needed to get the employees to see Braden's good side. If they could see that, they might be more cheerful and professional while on the job. And that, and not so much the food, was Priya's focus for this budding restaurant.

Still, her long-term goals would be pointless if she didn't perfect his execution. She looked up from her plate and compared it to his, which looked identical. She was pleased with herself right down to the carefully placed herbal garnish.

"C—can you show me what I did wrong?" Said a shaky voice to her right.

Priya looked up from the plates and saw the woman Braden had yelled at earlier. Her blue eyes were bloodshot and puffy from an apparent marathon crying session. Some of her short black hair clung to her cheeks, which were stained with tears.

"Sure. Why don't you get more quail, and we can start a new batch from scratch? I'm Priya, Priya Pant, by the way."

"Donna. Donna Brightman." Said the woman as she nodded with a weak smile.

Donna looked at what Priya was doing and followed until their plates mimicked each other.

"Perfect, Donna!" Priya said with a smile.

The kitchen door flung open. Braden walked through and headed straight towards them both. He looked at both plates, sampled them both, and nodded approval.

"Thanks for setting Donna straight, Priya."

Donna lowered her head and tiptoed to the prep station in the kitchen's corner to start on the asparagus for the salmon side dish. She let out a sigh. Braden followed Donna with his gaze as she walked over to the cutting board. He shook his head slightly and then turned his eyes to Priya.

"What's wrong with her? She's acting like I killed her cat." Braden said in a loud whisper.

"She's still upset about this morning."

"Why? It was a mistake—she corrected it, and we moved on."

"Braden, do you not remember your tone and all the foul language you used with her this morning?"

"Oh, for Christ's sake! I swear all the time. That's just who I am."

"It's an unbecoming tone for an employer." Said Priya as she frowned and shook her head.

"Oh, please, is Little Miss Prissy Priya going to tell me the error of my ways?"

Braden crossed his arms and puffed out his chest as he chuckled. Priya didn't want a choral repeat of this morning, so she narrowed her eyes and crossed her own arms in retort.

"For your information, my daddy was a preacher, and he taught us we didn't need to swear to get our point across to others. He also taught us not to name-call. You do realize that name-calling is a form of bullying, and you, sir, are acting like a child with all your elementary school comments." Priya let out a puff of breath. She couldn't believe she was sticking up for herself and the employees she and her boss shared this early in the game. But as his eyes softened to amusement levels, she grew angrier. "You know, I really thought I was getting through to you earlier when we were cooking the quail together. I guess I was wrong." She let out another breath. "It's like you've got a Jekyll and Hyde syndrome going on or something."

Braden's eyes widened, and his lips curled up before he let out a chuckle. This one was heartier than his first.

"Wow! I didn't think I hired a true Southern belle. This is going to be interesting." He laughed again before turning on his heel to head towards his office. "Very interesting, indeed. Hopefully, you can keep up with this Texas kitchen heat, Ms. Priya."

"What's that supposed to mean?"

Braden laughed again before closing the door to his office. She desperately wanted to run after him, giving him more pieces of her mind. The man clearly needed a good tongue lashing because he forgot the manners his momma, bless her heart, taught him. Of all the times she'd used the phrase, this was most likely the first time she was using it out of sympathy for a woman she only knew through the tabloids and media. A regal and proud woman whose eyes lit up with adoration whenever the papzz interviewed her about Brayden as a child. After a few seconds had passed and she slowed her breathing, she decided against following him. The only certainty of an action like that was her getting fired. And now, more than ever, she wanted to keep this job. If for no other reason, she was determined to keep it to show Mr. Bossypants that he couldn't get her goat!

REFERENCES

http://www.touregypt.net/featurestories/djet.htm
https://www.thecollector.com/ancient-egyptian-goddess-isis/
https://www2.kenyon.edu/Depts/Religion/Projects/Reln91/Power/lilith.htm
http://afe.easia.columbia.edu/cosmos/prb/heavenly.htm
https://www.amnh.org/explore/ology/archaeology/the-ancient-city-of-petra2
https://www.britannica.com/science/calendar/The-Egyptian-calendar
https://www.fragrancex.com/blog/fragrance-wheel/
http://www.candyhistory.net/candy-origin/first-candy/
https://www.archaeologynow.org/egypt-blog/blog-post-title-two-hz67c
https://destinationhistorypod.com/episodes/gobeklitepe

About the Author

USA Today Best Selling and award winning author Amanda Kimberley has written in various genres in the course of almost four decades.

Her nonfiction blog, which focuses on the chronic disease fibromyalgia, has garnered recognition from various organizations, including Health Magazine. Naming her blog, Fibro and Fabulous, as a top blog for fibro sufferers.

Amanda has also written for medical magazines

and sites like FM Aware, The National Fibromyalgia Association's magazine and ProHealth.

When Kimberley is not writing nonfiction, she enjoys penning romance. Her first Furry United Coalition story, The Turtle and the Hare, earned the 2020 Summer Splash Book Awards of Ink and Scratches for Best Romance. Her Forever Series Books, Forever Friends and Forever Bound were featured in 2015 and 2016 on the BookCountry website, a division of Penguin/Random House as editor's picks. She has also been featured as a USA Today Happy Ever After Hot List Indie Author with Claiming My Valentine, a Best Poet of the 90's ranking for an anthology, and has had a #1 PNR ranking with Immortal Hunger and Hearts Unleashed.

Amanda Kimberley is a Connecticut native that now lives in the warmth of Northern Texas with her zoo consisting of her husky, tuxedo cat, mice, rabbits, guinea pigs, a tank of fish, two daughters, and a husband.

When she is not writing you can find her cooking whole foods for her pack. She also enjoys reading, hiking, and gaming.

- facebook.com/authoramandakimberley
- twitter.com/KimberleyLB
- bookbub.com/profile/amanda-kimberley

Also by Amanda Kimberley

PNR Series

The Forever Series

Forever Friends

Forever Tied

Forever Cherished

Forever Bound

Forever Immortal

Forever Loved

Forever Blood

(Coming Soon)

Forever Yours

(Coming Soon)

Forever Mine

(Coming Soon)

Historical PNR Series

The Witch Journals Series

Salem's Trial by Judge

Salem's Trial by Township

Salem's Trial by Birth

(Coming Soon)

The Romani Witch Trials

(Coming Soon)

Colonial Witch Trials

(Coming Soon)

Stand Alone PNR

The Cure

Manifestations

Uncharted

The Pride Within

Co-Author Stand-Alone PNR

By the Pool with Alex Kimberley

Scifi Fantasy PNR

Suburban Shifter & Celestials Series

Loving the Alpha

Loving the Lone Wolf

Loving the Loup-garou

Loving the Rogue

Loving the Lykos

(Coming Soon)

The Equipoise Solar System Series

Laying Claim to the Lion

Laying Claim to the Legacy

Laying Claim to the Original

Laying Claim to the Dragon

(Coming Soon)

Laying Claim to the Leopard

(Coming Soon)

Laying Claim to the Panda

(Coming Soon)

Laying Claim to the Queen

(Coming Soon)

The Pandemic Series

Pandemic Passion

Pandemic Pandemonium

(Coming Soon)

The Midnight Rising Series

Midnight & Mistletoe

Midnight & Magic

Midnight & Memories

Midnight & Mergers

Midnight & Masquerades

RomCom PNR

The Eve L. Worlds Hellenic Island Shifter Series

The Turtle and the Hare

The Turtle and the Rock

The Ferret and the Fossa

The Leopard and the Llama

(Coming Soon)

Contemporary Romance
The Chronic Collection

Down by the Willow Tree

To Hell With Carpets

Welcome Home

The Chronic Collection

The Just Series

Just Breathe

Just Believe

(Coming Soon)

Just Be

(Coming Soon)

Nonfiction Self Help

The Fibro and Fabulous Series

Fibro and Fabulous: The Book

Fibromyalgia and Sex Can Be a Pain in the Neck

Fibromyalgia and Pregnancy

Poetry

Blue Water Baptism

The Puzzle Called Life

For More Information, Please Visit https://www.bookbub.com/profile/amanda-kimberley.

Milton Keynes UK
Ingram Content Group UK Ltd.
UKHW040719161023
430697UK00001B/28